"I'm sorry," Dash said.

"Why?" Raina quickly countered.

"Now you're in more danger and—"

"I chose to be here for my friend." She didn't need his pity.

"I still see it as my job to protect you, Raina."

"Why? You made it clear where we stand." She was baiting the bull out of her own fit of anger.

"Not because I don't care about you." He said the words low and under his breath to the point she barely heard them.

The reality of how dangerous his job was struck like a physical blow.

A surprising tear broke loose from Raina's eye and rolled down her cheek. This was exactly the reason she couldn't let her heart b̶̶̶̶̶̶̶̶̶̶̶̶̶̶̶̶̶̶̶̶̶r how perfect Da̶̶

He'd been clear̶

All my love to Brandon, Jacob and Tori,
the three great loves of my life.

To Babe, my hero, for being my best friend,
greatest love and my place to call home.

I love you all with everything that I am.

DECODING A CRIMINAL

USA TODAY Bestselling Author

BARB HAN

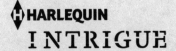

Special thanks and acknowledgment are given to Barb Han for her contribution to the Behavioral Analysis Unit miniseries.

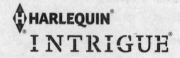

ISBN-13: 978-1-335-48902-9

Decoding a Criminal

Copyright © 2021 by Harlequin Books S.A.

Recycling programs for this product may not exist in your area.

This edition published by arrangement with Harlequin Books S.A.

For questions and comments about the quality of this book, please contact us at CustomerService@Harlequin.com.

Harlequin Enterprises ULC
22 Adelaide St. West, 40th Floor
Toronto, Ontario M5H 4E3, Canada
www.Harlequin.com

Printed in U.S.A.

USA TODAY bestselling author **Barb Han** lives in north Texas with her very own hero-worthy husband, three beautiful children, a spunky golden retriever/standard poodle mix and too many books in her to-read pile. In her downtime, she plays video games and spends much of her time on or around a basketball court. She loves interacting with readers and is grateful for their support. You can reach her at barbhan.com.

Visit the Author Profile page at Harlequin.com.

CAST OF CHARACTERS

Dashiell West (aka Dash)—This tech hotshot turned BAU agent will clear his sister if it's the last thing he does.

Raina Andress—Layla's best friend vows to prove her innocence.

Phish—This hacker is the one who set Layla up, but who is really hiding behind the code?

Layla West—This sister has a rough past, but does that predict future behavior?

Alec Kingsley—Layla's boss seems a little overeager to help. What is he hiding?

Natalia (Talia) Herzog—This ex can't leave Dash alone. Even a restraining order doesn't seem to scare her away.

Prologue

Click. Clack. Clack.

There was a special touch when it came to picking just the right keyboard. The mechanics were important. The sound, when heard over and over again, became melodic. Touch-type was critical. Less force made for better accuracy. Faster. More consistent. Same resistance all the way down. Keys were a little bit more uniform. Phish's fingers danced across the keyboard. Why wasn't the code working?

He stared at the vertical monitor directly in front of him in the temporary workspace he'd set up in the back of the late-night coffee shop he frequented. There were times in life, like this, when he preferred to be alone. No interruptions and no one looking over his shoulder.

Phish. He'd been given the nickname when he was young for his tech abilities. He'd thought it was funny. Now? Not so much, but it had stuck in certain circles no matter how hard he'd tried to shed it. Phish had lost count of how many lines of code he'd written, but the vertical monitor let him see more lines all at once. Made it easier to spot the problem. Usually.

The less scrolling, the better. He preferred to see as much of his masterpiece as possible. His cell phone to his left was parked on Google so he could troubleshoot while he wrote the key-logger program that would open the doors to the kingdom. Robbery was old fashioned, unsophisticated and for someone with an IQ of one hundred. Why go through all the trouble of physically walking into a building and waving a gun around when all Phish needed was a password? That was it. So much more…sophisticated. All he had to do was steal that magic string of characters, numbers and symbols. That was where the phishing came in; the way in which he could steal a password was through a virus that tracked all keystrokes on a computer and saved them, a.k.a. a key logger. To do that, he had to use a dummy laptop to run an operating system through a virtual machine. He used the dark café for their open Wi-Fi to hide where the data request came from. A trace would lead them to a coffee shop instead of his home network.

Once he installed the key-logger program, he could grab her passwords. That was all he needed to do to sneak two million dollars into an untraceable offshore account. The way he planned to do it made him smirk. Siphon a penny here, a penny there. Pennies added up in a large investment bank with millions of accounts. The account owners wouldn't even notice. No skin off their noses. Account holders never balanced their financial statement anymore. No one would miss a penny. He was doing them a favor, actually. This way, no one got hurt. No one ever missed paying rent over a penny, and the people in these accounts certainly wouldn't. Not one person would starve because they were one penny short on their grocery bill—no one's life hung in the balance over that small piece of copper.

The storefront he'd set up via the dark web would be the perfect cover to launder money into his accounts. Bringing the cash into the US in chunks would be the easy part—well…he thought about the word *easy*. Easy for him. Not for others. It wasn't his fault people were incompetent. Others weren't smart enough to pull off what Phish was capable of. He'd been underestimated and underappreciated his entire life. Guess what? Not anymore.

A little part of him wanted to take all the money from one account just to prove that he could. He wanted to shove his victory in their faces a little bit. Show them just how capable he was.

He stopped himself from going too far down that road. He was better than that. Smarter. They'd never catch him this way. They wouldn't even notice. No one noticed the little things. Everyone was too worried about making thousands of dollars off a trade to think about a penny.

Much like a ghost, he would be in and out before anyone ever realized what had hit them. Phish laughed, despite his eyes burning from staring at the screen too long. He always forgot to blink when he was this close to success.

Everything he had ever wanted was about to be his. He deserved this money after what he'd been through. He was owed this money. A cool two million was a good place to start for all the pain he'd endured from the bullies, from his parents. *Someone* might get in trouble for the missing money, but hey, as long as it wasn't him, he'd be cool with it.

Come on. Phish snatched the half-empty cup from the tabletop. The contents were tepid. He threw back the last of the drink. He needed the caffeine to kick in. Get his brain going again.

What was he missing?

He scanned the lines of code once more, starting from the top. Everything looked solid. His temper flared, and he squeezed the cup in his hand. *Think. Think.*

It shouldn't be this hard for him. This should be a smash-and-grab job without all the flair. Click. Clack. Clack.

Hold on. His gaze stopped halfway down the screen. *Is that the reason?*

No. Couldn't be that easy to fix. Could it?

Phish tapped the keys, remembering how much he'd hated the piano lessons he'd been forced into as a kid and how ironic it was he was about to become a millionaire after swearing off anything that had to do with a keyboard.

Funny how life worked. How it presented opportunities for the taking if someone was patient enough and smart enough to capitalize. Being fed up wasn't always bad.

He was getting closer. *Take the bait.*

No hard feelings to !qazxcde#. With a few keystrokes, Phish was in. Tomorrow night, when he came back, he'd have everything he ever wanted at his fingertips. Nervous excitement caused his hands to shake as he tapped the keys toward a better life. He was taking so little when he really thought about it, and yet, when piled together, it made so much. It was about time. He deserved this after everything he'd been through.

It was finally *his* time. And he was smart enough to take what was owed.

Chapter One

The FBI office was housed in a blue-glass skyscraper overlooking the Puget Sound just a couple of blocks from the Space Needle on Order Street. The BAU covered the top floor, lucky number forty-two.

"Welcome. Thank you for coming on short notice." Supervisory special agent Miguel Peters took a seat last in the conference room at BAU headquarters. "You've all read the headlines by now involving our very own Special Agent Dashiell West's sister, Layla. Some of you have already started working on the case. Dash has a few items to speak to, so I'll turn the meeting over to him." Miguel held out his hand like he was presenting a new car.

"Right. Thank you." Dashiell West, known as Dash to friends and colleagues, was in no mood to waste time. He knew everyone in the room: Nicholas James, who specialized in serial killers; kidnapping expert Madeline Striker; tech guru Liam and his fiancée, Lorelai, who was the BAU's director's assistant. "As you are all aware by now, the media has been having a field day with my sister's arrest."

"Shouldn't have gone down that way." Nicholas smacked his flat palm against the conference table. "Hasn't anyone heard of professional courtesy?"

"It's not every day a hedge fund manager and sister of a cybercrime expert/FBI special agent embezzles two million dollars." Dash blew out a slow breath as he searched the faces in the room. "A heads-up to the department before the arrest would have been nice, even though the crime isn't exactly sneaking a few twenties out the petty cash drawer."

"Any chance they believe you're somehow involved or at least looked the other way?" Liam asked.

"It's possible. You'd have to ask the boss here. I'm guessing he would be their first stop." Dash rubbed the scruff on his chin. "But it doesn't matter. I'm clean and it won't take long for them to figure it out."

"News reports said the money isn't in any of Layla's personal accounts, so why do they believe she's involved, other than the obvious fact her password was used?" Nicholas asked.

"The money was siphoned off her clients' accounts via an IP address that leads to a coffee shop here in Seattle. It's a known hangout for programmers and offers a lot of privacy for late-night clients. It's been tied to activity on the dark web, and everyone who knows my sister knows her hobby is cracking the dark web," Dash said. "She also frequents that coffee shop, so employees identified her. There are ways to scour offshore accounts, particularly so early in the embezzlement, but no one can find the money. Money is missing. Her password was used. Usually, that means law enforcement has found their person."

"I heard the cash was moved in trace amounts across a lot of accounts," Liam said.

Dash nodded.

"Brilliant, if you ask me." With Liam's technical background, he would understand Layla the best, aside from Dash himself.

He couldn't help but think the description of the crime fit his sister. The others had to be thinking it too. If Layla was going to pull something like that, she would have done it exactly the same way. A middle finger to the system. But her life was good. She'd distanced herself from her past, had a job that more than covered her lifestyle. She lived in a nice apartment on a high floor with a view of the Needle. Did she like the finer things in life? Yes. But she would never use her own password.

"Don't you have to have the evidence in order to arrest someone?" Liam's question was rhetorical.

"The missing money and Layla's password is the only connection they seem to need to make the arrest stick." Dash agreed, though.

"Too obvious." Liam shook his head, then drummed his fingers on the conference table.

"We all know the evidence usually leads us to the right criminal. Law Enforcement 101," Miguel interjected.

"She's smarter than that." *And has more of a sense of humor*, Dash thought. She would put a signature stamp on it. Something to make that flick off stick up and stay up.

Despite this feeling, he was 90 percent certain this wasn't his sister's doing. Maybe that was a lowball number. Ninety-three percent, because last month he'd accused her of speeding in the new Porsche she bought, and he'd been wrong. She'd proved it with a speeding app on her phone. Probability said he was bound to be wrong at some point.

"How much is that apartment she lives in?" Someone had to ask the question. Miguel clasped his hands together and his face muscles pulled taut.

"A lot." Dash wasn't the least bit defensive. It was gospel truth: Layla had champagne taste.

He'd been a hotshot at a Tech firm once, and had been plucked out of IT and dropped straight into app development. In five years, he'd applied for eleven patents—a company record. He'd decided to walk away and develop software on his own. After hitting it big, he bought out the noncompete lawsuit and banked enough cash to get him through several lifetimes. There was a point when money just became zeroes in a bank account. They didn't change someone's worth or make the person better than anyone else. But money did give freedom, and that was how Dash could afford to live in an apartment like this, drive any car he desired and still work in a job that paid less than what he was used to paying in taxes from his software income.

"She likes nice things. Doesn't make her a criminal." Lorelai, who'd been quiet up to now, threw her hands up in the air.

"And she wouldn't use her own password," Liam insisted.

"The other problem, once investigators started looking into Layla's personal computer, is that they discovered how much she loves the dark web." His sister was also brilliant enough to outsmart the system. If she had taken the money—and he wasn't saying she had—making herself a target would also mean she'd be investigated and released early in the process. Now that he really thought about it, sticking it to the system might be implicating herself and then proving she didn't do it.

"I heard about her affinity for all things dark on the web." Lorelai's arms were crossed over her chest, her expression serious. She could be the poster child for the FBI, in her navy pantsuit and shoulder holster. In fact, he was pretty sure she'd been asked. "Let's talk about a hacker's psychology for a second."

"A hacker is someone who is manipulative, deceitful, exploitative, cynical and insensitive," Madeline supplied. "Generally driven by a need for peer recognition and respect."

"That doesn't describe Layla," Liam stated.

"My sister wouldn't take other people's money." Dash hoped the decisiveness in his voice and the fact that he didn't hesitate in his response would win his sister a few points with Lorelai. He'd spent the last couple of days trying to track down the unsub on his own, without any luck. He'd asked his boss for time off from work, but Miguel declined the request. Said Dash would get further using BAU resources than he would on his own. The rub? They would look at the case like she was guilty.

"Will she give us unfettered access to all her devices?" Lorelai asked. Her eyebrow arched.

"I can ask her." Dash figured the answer would be a resounding *hell no*. He'd figure out a way to convince Layla. No choice there. And he wasn't just talking about the technology issued by her job—she would have her own devices.

"Just to be clear—your sister is presently incarcerated," Lorelai clarified.

"Yes, ma'am." The *ma'am* bit was probably unnecessary. It wasn't her favorite term. Lorelai must have gotten the message, as her back straightened a little more.

"Clear me from all other cases. I feel that I'm in a position to help Dash the most," Liam announced.

Lorelai shot a look at Liam that would freeze hell over. Dash hadn't meant to add to the tension brewing between them with his own problem: a sister he needed to figure out how to rein in as much as he needed to save. But then, he'd been trying to protect Layla ever since their parents died.

"I've met your sister. I have enough coffee to keep me going for a couple of days." Liam cracked his knuckles. "You can count on any and all of the tech skills I have to help free Layla."

His fiancée shot daggers at him. She pursed her

lips together and dropped her gaze to the wooden table.

"Has your sister pissed anyone off lately?" Nicholas had been quiet up to this point.

"As in, someone who would want to set her up?" Dash asked.

"That's exactly what I was thinking. We all know she wouldn't be stupid or clumsy enough to hand over her passwords to anyone," Nicholas surmised.

"I plan to visit her to ask. But she hasn't mentioned anyone." A wave of guilt washed over Dash. He should have known more about his sister's personal life. She'd been quiet lately, and it was all too easy for him to get busy with his own life. *Life?* He almost laughed out loud. *Work* might be a better word choice.

"Could be someone in her office who wanted her job or had it in for her," Nicholas said.

"That's an angle worth exploring." Dash nodded. He stared at the manila folder sitting in front of him. "Since you're all investigating my sister—" he put his forefingers and thumbs on the corners of the folder and then pushed it toward the center of the table "—you should know about her past."

Everyone stared at it for a long moment like it was a bomb about to detonate. Liam made the first move. He opened the folder.

"She has a juvie record?" Liam closed the file. "Wouldn't that record be sealed?"

"Not in this room, it isn't." They needed her history to create the best-possible profile on her. Do that and they would learn the way she thought. Learn the way she thought, and they could come at this from her perspective. "Open it."

On a sharp sigh, Liam picked up the manila folder and then opened it again.

"Go ahead," Dash urged. "Read it out loud so everyone can hear."

"Is that really—"

"Yes. If you're going to help, you need to know her past."

"She works in the financial industry. Don't they perform background checks?" Lorelai asked.

"Good question. Layla hacked into the juvenile justice system and finagled her records. The one in Liam's hands is probably the only correct piece of information you'll ever find. That's the reason you need to hear it. See it. Memorize it. When I leave this room, it goes with me and that's the last you'll ever see of it."

"She spent time in juvie for petty burglary at sixteen years old," Liam noted.

"That's right." Dash wasn't one for words and he'd already spoken more than he cared to in a day. A dull ache was forming behind his eyes. And this day was just getting started. "Our dad died in a car crash. Things got out of hand at home. Layla went down a bad path and got herself into trouble. She started with small stuff and moved up to petty burglary, which is when she got caught."

"Everyone processes pain differently," Liam said defensively.

"Yes. But not everyone acts out by committing a crime." Dash hadn't been there for her in the way he should have been.

"Your sister is a good person," Liam stated.

"I won't disagree with you there. She became a handful in her teen years, and I'm lucky all she got caught for was the burglary."

"Is that when you stepped into the picture?" Liam asked.

"Yes." Dash had inherited his very sullen, very bullheaded younger sister, who came to him cool on the surface and a mess underneath. She had more walls erected than a construction site. Dash wasn't so great with words, which made helping her that much more challenging.

"How'd she turn it around?" Miguel asked.

"I did for her what the military did for me. Gave her structure and enough physical work every day for her to flop into bed every night exhausted. Then I'd drag her out of bed every morning before the sun for a workout." Dash hadn't known what to do with her emotions. She wasn't one to talk either. No sitting up all night braiding hair at sleepovers for that kid. All he knew was physical labor, and she had responded to it.

"You have my assurance that if your sister is innocent—and we have to operate as though she may not be—we'll find the proof and clear her name," Miguel said. "In the meantime, keep us up to date with everything you find."

"Yes, sir." The *may not be* echoed in Dash's head.

As far as probabilities went, he was 96 percent certain Layla was innocent. It was the 4 percent that worried him. His baby sister had always had that edge to her, and he'd gone through hell and back to get her on the right side of the law when she was sixteen. The 4 percent that would keep him awake at night was that Layla really did like the finer things. She'd been keeping to herself lately. Secretive. Something was going on with her and, again, he'd had no idea how to approach the subject with her.

As the room cleared, Dash had another realization. Dammit, he was going to need to talk to Raina Andress—not only was she Layla's BFF but she was also a tech guru. She must be trying to clear Layla, too, and he needed all hands on deck for this assignment. Plus, he didn't want them accidentally tripping over each other or duplicating work.

After what had happened between them, would she even talk to him? He could swing by her office and try to force her into a conversation. She worked at the same firm as Layla, just in a different department. Dash picked up the manila folder and stuffed it inside his jacket. Raina wasn't going to be happy about seeing him again. He'd made sure of it during their last conversation.

First up, though, he needed to speak to Layla's boss.

RAINA ANDRESS'S HEELS clicked against the marble tiles of the bank's lobby as she crossed the room. The four-story lobby and floor-to-ceiling windows had always looked sophisticated to her in the past. Walking across the room and past the security desk to the bank of elevators had always made her feel like she'd made it to exactly where she wanted to be by age thirty-one. The opulence reminded her that her life was on track.

A café to her left, tucked on the side of the lobby, that served all the popular lattes was where she'd spent countless hours in meetings. Like the aftermath of a rock being thrown through a window, her world had come crashing down around her when her best friend, Layla West, was arrested for embezzlement. Now, she looked at everyone in the building with suspicion. She was reminded how fragile glass could be.

Considering it was common knowledge the two were close, Raina's career didn't have solid footing. An internal security investigation that led to her boss checking her computer revealed she wasn't involved. But neither was Layla. Raina would bet her life savings on her friend's innocence.

Halfway across the lobby, the hairs on the back of her neck prickled. Out of the corner of her eye, she saw a linebacker of a man leaning against the glass. He wasn't more than a shadow in dark pants and a collared shirt. On first blush, she thought he might be FBI.

She shouldn't look. She reminded herself not to do anything that might come across as an invitation to talk to her. All she wanted was to get past security without making a scene and slip inside the elevator.

Her heart thumped so loudly there was no way everyone in the bustling lobby didn't hear it. And then it dawned on her. She knew why the figure seemed familiar. He had a name: Dashiell West. No amount of security could keep him out of the building.

Raina picked up the pace. The click of her expensive heels echoed through the lobby. Dash was making a beeline toward her, so she hurried.

The timing would have to be perfect, but hey, miracles happened. Right? She barked out a laugh. Not for her, they didn't.

In a stroke of luck, she hopped onto an elevator just as she heard the swish behind her.

"Wait." Even the man's voice caused her arms to goose bump. His deep timbre traveled all over her body, bringing parts to life she couldn't afford to acknowledge.

With a whoosh, the doors closed.

"Ha."

She realized she must have said it out loud since all five people in the elevator turned toward her.

Raina gripped her computer bag. She always carried her laptop with her to and from work. She never knew when she'd need access to the sensitive files that were kept only on this device. Not even with all the encryption in the world could some of these files be shared over a network or stored in a cloud.

She tightened her grip on the laptop case and got off the elevator on seven. She stepped off long enough for the doors to close before pushing the down button, figuring she could face Dash another time. Maybe when she could get her traitorous body to stop lusting for her best friend's brother.

The elevator door opened, and she stepped on. Alone inside, she breathed a sigh of relief, knowing full well Dashiell West was on his way up to the thirty-third floor. No one needed that kind of negativity in life.

Their last conversation had left a lot to be desired. She was still trying to erase it from her mind. Raina shivered, shaking it off. She punched the button to the building's fifth-floor cafeteria. She could work there until Dash gave up and went home. She had nothing to say to him.

Chapter Two

"Thank you for agreeing to meet with me." Dash shook the outstretched hand of his sister's boss, which was cold and clammy, and left a strange feeling on Dash's palm. He tucked his own hand back inside his pocket to hide the fact that he wiped it off.

"Anything I can do to cooperate with the FBI's investigation and help your sister. You can count on help from my office in any way you need." Alec Kingsley seemed a little overeager. Dash had seen this kind of enthusiasm before but usually in guilty people trying to cover for themselves. "Come on in and have a seat."

"I'd rather stand, if it's okay with you." Dash followed Alec inside. The man needed to know who was in charge of this meeting. What could Dash say? Subtlety wasn't his strong suit unless he needed it to be. He took a half step inside the room, folded his arms over his chest and then leaned back against the wall.

"Make yourself comfortable, Special Agent West." Alec had one of those smiles—perfect white teeth that looked like they'd spent more years in braces than out during his high school years. He wore a thousand-dollar suit, and Dash would bet money he'd gone to a prep school somewhere in the Northeast. His shirt was tailored. Off the rack would never do for someone with the last name Kingsley.

"Thank you." Dash needed to feel the guy out. He glanced around the corner office and at the floor-to-ceiling windows. There were trophies lined up on a glass table pushed up against one wall. Fishing. Hunting. An oversized fish paperweight sat prominently on his desk. There were pictures of Alec with his arm around today's hottest celebrities against the backdrop of charity events and golf tournaments. Celebs weren't the only crowd Alec spent time with. There was a photo of him on horseback next to a prince who looked to be kicking off hunting season. There were a few other photos too. Ones of Alec with his arm around top-of-the-charts musicians and others with widely known organized crime tie-ins.

The guy was connected.

The black marble-tile flooring must've set the company back a pretty penny, not to mention the view. Hadn't Layla said the buy-in for her hedge fund was a cool two million? The exact amount in question. How was that for a middle finger?

"I have been personally devastated by the news of Layla's arrest," Alec said, and he genuinely looked the part. "I just can't imagine her doing anything like that after all the opportunities she's been given here."

"How would you classify your working relationship with Layla West?" Dash didn't figure he'd get the truth out of Alec, but he could tell a lot from the kind of lies he told.

"Good. She's one of the best on my team." Alec delivered the line with a silk tongue. He had one of those smiles meant to disarm. Smooth and sophisticated. Dash bet the man could turn on his prep school dazzle and charm the skin off a snake.

"Any disagreements? Insubordination?"

"No. Nothing like that." Alec waved his hand in the air. Instead of walking around to the other side of his desk and claiming his spot, he perched on the edge of his seat and folded his arms. His torso was tilted slightly toward Dash. These were behaviors that showed Alec was listening and interested in what Dash had to say. Arms crossed over the chest usually signaled someone was holding back or covering, Dash thought for a second time in a matter of minutes.

Layla wouldn't be naive enough to give away her password to anyone, including her boss. She'd set up a back door and track him rather than give her personal password away. The dark web had to be involved in some way. Plus, the IP address had been traced to the café, so…

Alec and the dark web?

There were other explanations for his body language. He could be nervous and trying to cover. Most people were a little on edge after he'd identified himself. Alec might not be guilty of stealing Layla's password, but he could be concerned about something else. Nothing scared off investors like the threat of a federal investigation.

"You know what, though?" The muscles in Alec's face tensed.

Dash shrugged.

"Thinking back, Layla has been different lately."

"Different how?" All he needed was this guy testifying how her personality had recently changed to put another nail in Layla's coffin.

Alec rubbed his clean-shaven chin. "Little things. She's been quiet."

If Layla didn't have anything to say to someone, quiet was her default setting. *Quiet* wasn't a crime.

"More so than normal?" Dash asked. He wanted more details.

"It's more than quiet. Maybe that's not the right word. *Moody* might be a better way to describe her."

Dash rolled his eyes. He couldn't help himself. "Moodier than usual?"

"Yes. I'd say."

Like a storm brewing off the Atlantic, Layla could be tempestuous. It generally meant she'd gone to that dark place again. The space inside her head that sometimes trapped her in a prison of bad memories—memories that she refused to discuss to this day, even with her brother. Losing their mother at a young age had been hard on her. Surviving the car crash that killed their father haunted her.

And hell on a stick, she'd landed in juvie once before after one of those storms.

"What else? Was her work slipping?" he asked.

"Never. She was always on top of her game. We have a fairly flexible work-from-home policy, and she's been working remotely more than usual. When she came into the office, she didn't have her typical sharpness to her appearance."

Custom suits. Thousand-dollar shoes. He didn't even want to know how much she spent on straightening her natural curls at a salon, but she had a regular weekly appointment. Don't even get him started on the maintenance her nails required. How on earth could she look anything but crisp?

Besides, appearances meant a lot to his baby sister. Dash had been shorted that gene. Unless he had to dress up for work, he was most comfortable in jeans and a cotton T-shirt.

"When you say 'moody,' what do you mean, exactly? Did she jump down your throat for saying hello before she had coffee or completely ignore everyone?"

Alec nodded as Dash spoke, and for some odd reason, it burned him up. His protective instincts had always been in overdrive when it came to Layla. He hoped his flaw didn't turn out to be fatal.

"Yeah." He drew out the word. "I'd say secretive. Keeping to herself more when she was in the office."

He wouldn't classify Layla as outgoing by any stretch of the word. Smart bordering on brilliant? No question there. The meeting with her high school AP Calculus teacher came to mind. Mrs. Tudor had been failing Layla despite the fact that she rarely missed a problem on homework or a test. The problem, according to Mrs. Tudor, was that Layla didn't show her work.

Layla shrugged. "It slows me down and, guess what, I don't need it," he remembered her saying.

Dash's response still made him proud to this day. He'd leaned back in his chair and rubbed his face with his hands, then said, "If you continue to punish my sister because she—"

"Oh, no. No. That's not what's happening here." Mrs. Tudor's cheeks puffed out and her face turned red. She resembled a teakettle about to explode. "She has to follow the steps just like everyone. That's how you learn math."

"Then let's make a deal." He raised his voice enough to get the older woman's attention. *Old school* didn't begin to describe her looks, and her tactics were just as bad. "You can take points off for every problem my sister gets wrong. But if the answer is right, you give her full credit. If she fails math, you won't see or hear from me again. Period. I won't go to the principal and complain about your inability to teach. I won't go to the school board to complain about your teaching methods." He made air quotes around the word *teaching*.

"Well, I suppose if she gets the answer correct… I could see how not everyone would have to…" She stopped right there and made a face as though her brain couldn't fathom someone just being able to solve the problem mentally without all the steps. "She won't be able to receive partial credit."

"Nope. Doesn't need it." He'd checked over her

problems meticulously. She'd done them correctly. Rarely did she mess up. "Do I have your agreement?"

Mrs. Tudor seemed to be doing a few calculations of her own. How much trouble would he cause? That was X in the equation. He must've looked like trouble, because she finally blew out a sharp breath and threw her hands up in the air. "If the answer is correct and she isn't using an aid like a calculator or watch, then—"

"Why don't you believe me? I don't have to cheat." Layla had smacked the desk with the flat of her hand. She had patience the size of a purse dog's bladder.

Mrs. Tudor gasped. Her hand came up to her mouth.

"Not the time, Layla," Dash warned.

She exhaled in the kind of dramatic fashion reserved for teenagers.

"Fine," Layla said.

"Fine," Mrs. Tudor echoed. "We have an understanding."

That had been the last time he saw his sister's math teacher. But Dash was still sticking up for his baby sister.

The memory had played out in his head fast, but by the time he refocused on Alec, the man looked bored.

"Can I have access to Layla's work computer?" Dash figured it was worth a try.

"You can expect our full cooperation, Mr. West. We here at Baker Financial pride ourselves on discretion. Our clients demand it and we wouldn't be in business without it. I'm happy to answer any questions but…"

"I'll do everything in my power to get to the bottom of the investigation." Dash wanted to remind Alec that his sister's very public firing wasn't what he would consider *flying under the radar*.

"We've already provided access to investigators. Perhaps you could work with the other agency," Alec said.

Dash's hands fisted at his sides. Since he didn't have a warrant, he nodded. So much for full cooperation.

"Unfortunately, confidentiality agreements between the firm and our clients prevent me from being of much help. My assistant can escort you to the lobby now." He leaned back and pressed an intercom button. "Mr. West is ready to leave."

Knowing when to push forward and when to retreat was the art of an investigation. Dash's skills at reading a situation were top notch. This was the time to back off and regroup. They were in the early stages of the investigation and would get further with cooperation from Layla's boss. *Former boss*, he corrected.

"I appreciate your cooperation. Someone from my office will be in touch." Dash extended his right hand. The clammy feeling struck again with their contact. Jenny, the perky assistant, greeted him at the door.

"Right this way, sir." Jenny was blond and beautiful. Her clothes fit her curves—curves she knew how to work as she walked in front of Dash. A person like Jenny was a distraction to the millions of dollars being won and lost on this floor. The amounts were staggering, when Dash really thought about it.

Other than his penthouse apartment and expensive car, the fanciest he ever got in his day-to-day life was taking his cold beer in a bottle instead of a can. Nothing imported either. Cold glass. Good beer.

"Thank you for stopping by today." Jenny turned around and he could've sworn he caught her eyeing him up and down, her gaze lingering on his chest. An invitation? Or was Jenny this friendly to everyone they were trying to distract?

Dash let himself be walked to the elevator. Jenny pressed the down button for him. For a brief moment, he thought about all the times a young Layla had raced to an elevator to be the one to push the button. There were ten years between them, and the decade caused them to have two very different upbringings after the loss of their father. Had Dash done the right things for Layla?

"Have a wonderful day." Jenny leaned toward him enough to give him a peek at her generous breasts. She discreetly slipped something in his hand.

"Same to you." The slip of paper went inside his pocket right before he pushed the *L*.

As soon as the doors closed, he changed his mind and hit the fifth floor button. Since Alec didn't send Dash out with a security guard, he figured he could play around in the building to see what he could come up with. Besides, there was a conversation he still needed to have and he highly doubted Raina had gone to her office after making eye contact in the lobby.

He glanced at the paper Jenny handed him…found her number.

The elevator doors opened on five. It was his lucky day. Raina Andress sat on the other side of a glass wall in the cafeteria. And his luck had doubled down—she was facing sideways so that he could see her profile perfectly. His traitorous heart clenched at seeing her again. But this wasn't a social call.

Chapter Three

Click. Clack. Clack.

Raina's fingers were zinging across the mechanical keys on her keyboard. It was strangely musical when this happened and incredibly satisfying. She could get lost in the sound; she was having one of those moments that some people described as being *in the zone.*

She was close to a breakthrough. She could feel it. Right up until the moment the hairs on the back of her neck prickled with the sensation that someone was watching her.

Glancing up and around, she massaged her stiff neck with her right hand. The moment her eyes landed on him, her hand dropped and her heart squeezed. Panic made her shirt suddenly feel three sizes too small.

She closed her laptop and fumbled for the plug. She'd forgotten to charge it last night, making a smooth exit impossible.

Her fingers closed around the plug as she felt the

physical presence that was Dashiell West standing next to her.

"Not today, Dash." She crammed the cord into her backpack, then the laptop itself in the quilted section.

"We need to talk."

"Oh yeah? *We* aren't very good at it. So no thanks." She stood up, thinking he'd back away a step or two. Boy, was she wrong. All she ended up doing was breathing in his spicy masculine scent. Her body betrayed her with an attraction that could pull a magnet out of orbit.

"I'm sorry."

She issued a sharp sigh. "That's below the belt."

"What if I mean it?"

"I didn't think you could go any lower than the initial apology." She tried to step around him but found herself penned in. "Move."

He took a step back and held one of those muscled arms in the air like he was showing her the way. Well, that really made her mad. He didn't get to tell her when to make an exit. *Keep cool, Raina.*

She had no idea where that voice came from. Now she was talking to herself?

Taking in a slow, measured breath, she moved a couple of steps away from Dash, mostly to put enough space between them to let go of some of her anger and, frankly, for her brain to function clearly again.

"Why are you here?" The minute the question left her mouth, she wished she could reel it back in. Because standing out of the vortex that was all things

Dash, she realized exactly why he was here in her temporary workspace. The question she should be asking was how he found her in the cafeteria.

"Layla." They said his sister and her best friend's name at the exact same moment. Not the time to prove they were in sync on anything, she thought.

"Do you have time to grab a cup of coffee?" Worry lines scored Dash's forehead.

"Now?"

"Yes."

"Are you asking me out on a date?" She should have held her tongue. Turned out, she wasn't so good at it.

"Raina, can we set…" Even his eyes seemed to be searching for a diplomatic response. "…*that* aside and come back to it once my sister is released?"

Oh, the moment of truth had finally arrived. Did she love her best friend more than her own pride? Well, that was a yes. She would do anything to clear Layla. Scratch that. *Almost* anything. Could she work with a man she despised?

"Yes." She was most likely going to live to regret her decision. But, yes, she would do whatever needed to happen for Layla. "To be clear, this is for Layla and has nothing to do with our…history."

"Crystal." Dash had the most intense eyes—dark, like in a strangely earthy but also untouchable sense. "The offer of coffee is strictly because I need to get out of the building before security realizes I never made it to the lobby."

She must've shot him a strange look.

"I just met with Layla's boss."

"Alec Kingsley?"

"He seemed pretty ready to send me on my way."
Dash's gaze focused on someone or something behind her.

She turned in time to see a uniformed guard wearing his cranky face, making a beeline toward them.
She might hate herself for doing this later, but…

"Oh, Dash." She took hold of his arm, regretting
the second she made contact with his body. There
was enough electricity pinging between them to
power a small island. "Thanks for letting me grab
you for a few minutes to show you around. We're
late, so we better go."

The tension lines bracketing Dash's lips eased.
His tongue darted across those full lips, leaving a
silky trail that Raina had no business staring at.

"Excuse me, ma'am." Luis Meter looked ready to
throw Dash down face-first onto the marbled floor.
As much as she'd pay good money to see that happen, she also realized Luis would lose. Dash may
have come from the tech world, but he grew up playing multiple sports and had a black belt in kung fu.
The man was in tip-top condition, whereas Luis's
shape could best be described as *round*. Round with
a ruddy face. He would be strong, though.

"Hi." Raina did her best to play the confused girlfriend part. "Can I help you, Luis?"

"Do you know this man?"

"Oh. Yes. If you're talking about Special Agent

Dashiell West, then I do." She squeezed his arm, ignoring the way her heart pounded against her rib cage.

Luis's eyes widened enough to give away the fact that he was impressed by Dash's title—exactly what she was going for. Throwing him off-balance was the play.

"We were just about to leave. He was on his way down and I stopped him. There was no way I was letting my old friend walk out of my workplace without catching up first. We're heading around the corner to that new place for a decent breakfast, so if you don't mind." She blinked at him. "Or did you need him for something else?"

"No, ma'am. In fact, I came to escort Mr., uh, Special Agent West out of the building per Mr. Kingsley's request." Luis took a step back to allow them to pass. "I'd be happy to walk you both out."

"Great. Thank you." She tugged on Dash's arm, forcing him to follow Luis.

In the elevator, she cozied up to Dash. Luis's face flushed like he was intruding on an intimate moment when she leaned in to whisper in Dash's ear.

"I can't believe it's been so long since we've seen each other," she said softly, using as sexy a voice as she could muster. Sexy voice had never been her thing, so it was awkward, but she pushed through the embarrassment. "I'm glad you're here now, though."

Dash didn't respond. In fact, his face broke into a wide smile, and he wasn't helping matters.

Finally, the elevator made it to the lobby and the

doors opened. Luis put his hand in the door to stop it from closing.

"Ma'am." He didn't look at her when he said it.

They filed out and he followed closely behind. Her heels clicked against the marble flooring and, once again, she noticed the hollow sound to the echo.

As soon as they got outside, she let go of his arm.

"What was that supposed to be back there?" The tone of his voice sounded a lot like disapproval.

"Excuse me? I was helping you." She tried to stop walking, but his hand on her lower back urged her to continue.

"Remind me not to ask for help from you in the future. Next time, leave it to me," he ground out.

"So you can stand there and do nothing? No thanks."

"I didn't want to embarrass you by cutting into the routine you had going there."

"Hold on a minute." Raina had a temper, and it was flaring. She was going to say something she regretted. What was she supposed to do instead of speak her mind? Because at thirty-one years old, she was still trying to learn that lesson.

Stop, look and listen? No. That was crossing the street.

Stop, drop and roll? Nope. Learned that move from the fire department.

How about this one: count to ten, with slow breaths in between. Bingo.

The last one helped, and she humored herself in

the process, breaking up a bit of the tension that caused sharp pains in her shoulder blades.

"How did you think you were going to embarrass me when I was the only one doing anything?" she asked in as calm a voice as she could muster.

"First of all, you were overexplaining." Dash liked his hand on the small of Raina's back a helluva lot more than he should.

"What does that mean, exactly?" She blinked at him, clearly confused.

"Going into too many details is the first sign of someone lying."

"No, it isn't," she countered.

So, now she was going to tell him about his job? Didn't she realize he studied body language as part of his profession? His training involved spotting liars. He didn't respond right away because she was too mad. It was causing her to speak before she had a chance to think, be defensive when he needed to gain her cooperation. And, apparently, the fact that he was trying to help her was just making her more frustrated with him.

She blew out a sharp breath. She'd been doing that a lot today, he noticed.

"Okay. Fine. I overexplained. I don't think Luis was smart enough to catch on, though. He's not highly trained like you are. His training probably consisted of watching a few videos, and he might watch movies like *Die Hard*. In case you didn't notice, he wasn't in the best of shape, physically."

"I notice everything." His statement wasn't meant to make her blush, but the rosy hue only made her more beautiful.

"What else did I do wrong?"

"The whole acting-surprised bit. We usually see that as a sign someone is covering up for something."

"I *was* covering for you."

"Believe it or not, I can handle myself. I've gotten into some sticky situations with my job and managed to get out of them just fine on my own."

"I thought you asked me to breakfast in order to get my help."

He diverted them into a hotel lobby.

"Hold on a minute." Raina stopped abruptly, realizing exactly where they'd just entered.

"Don't get the wrong idea. I picked this place because no one knows about the coffee shop in this little corner. Also, I happen to know it's not bugged." An unwanted stab of disappointment came out of nowhere. Dash didn't want to feel regret when he thought about Raina, but that's exactly what happened.

Chapter Four

The coffee shop was empty, save for a couple of employees. And not for nothing, but that was one of the many reasons he loved the place. He and his sister had met up there a handful of times. The café itself occupied a dark corner.

Dash remembered the slip of paper he'd tucked into his pocket with Jenny's number on it. He reached inside, palmed it and brought it out on the down-low. Risking a glance while Raina ordered, he saw Jenny's name and number scribbled down. Nothing more. With the way she'd been flirting with him, his first guess was that she was fishing for a date. The investigator in him also had to consider the flirting was an act. She wouldn't be able to speak freely in front of her boss, and she might have information or suspicions she wanted to discuss.

He'd take a hard pass if she was hitting on him, but not if she had information that could aid his investigation and help Layla.

"What can I get working for you today, sir?" the perky barista practically chirped. He recognized her as someone he'd seen there several times before. It had been a while since he'd been back. Dash thought about the comment Alec had made about Layla working from home recently.

He tucked the piece of paper back inside his pocket and stepped forward. As he opened his mouth to speak, the barista blushed and held up her hand to stop him.

"Black coffee. Haven't seen you in a while." Her gaze immediately dropped to the register as she bit down on her bottom lip so hard it might bleed.

Dash paid for both orders and then moved to the left.

"See you again soon." The hope in the barista's voice seemed to irritate Raina. She clucked her tongue, as if to say *the nerve*.

This was probably not the time to regret the night the two of them had spent together. Actually, *regret* wasn't the right word for a night of the best sex he'd ever had. Regret came the next day, when both seemed to realize their fling couldn't go anywhere. It had been doomed from the start, and now they were in a precarious position. Layla was going to flip when she found out He'd had sex with her best friend on Layla's birthday.

Dash had been the one to voice it to Raina. Heated words were exchanged. Had he been a jerk? Looking back, he could've handled the situation better.

Neither spoke while waiting for their orders to be called out. The barista worked at a leisurely pace. Normally, he'd appreciate someone taking the time to get an order right and do a good job. Today, he just wanted to get his coffee, sit down and get to business. Alec's comment about his sister letting her appearance go kept eating away at the back of Dash's mind.

Layla was on a good path. She had a nice apartment with nice things. Clothes. He had to wonder what incentive she would have to risk it all and take the money. Going down that path was inevitable because blindly following the road where there was no way she would do it was the surest way to miss something that might be critical. He had to put all his brotherly instincts on hold and force objectivity.

"Drip for Dash." The barista chuckled at the alliteration.

Dash wasn't as amused. He grabbed his coffee from the granite counter where it had been placed.

"I'll save you the trouble. The next one's mine," Raina quipped. She didn't seem impressed by the guy either. Her no-nonsense approach to life had been one of her many draws. But this wasn't the time or the place to ruminate over her long list of attractive qualities. When she gave a half smile to the barista as he set her drink down, the guy winked.

Without realizing it, Dash fisted his free hand. He forced himself to relax as Raina scooped up her drink, seemingly unaffected by the flirtation. Dash exhaled slowly. The barista was trying his patience.

"Where would you like to sit?" Out of habit, Dash kept the workers in view as he pivoted in the opposite direction. He was used to sizing up every person in the room and memorizing exits. This was no exception. His area of expertise might be tech, but he was a trained field agent capable of taking a person down using physical or deadly force if the situation called for either, which basically meant always being watchful and alert.

"Here's good." Raina chose a spot in the back of the room, out of the baristas' listening range.

Dash held out a chair for her, forcing her back to the room. He took the opposite seat so he'd have a full view.

"Are you officially investigating—" she glanced around and lowered her voice "—your sister's case?"

"Yes."

"They let you?" She raised an eyebrow, surprised.

"Not so much as resigned themselves to the fact I was going to do it anyway. This way, Miguel gets updates from me and can keep an eye on the PR nightmare this is turning into." He took a sip of coffee, enjoying the burn on his throat.

"Makes sense, actually." She tucked a loose tendril of hair behind her right ear. Then she blew out a breath, and her torso resembled a balloon deflating. "I haven't slept in longer than I can count. Not since I found out about what happened." She flashed her eyes at him. This close, he could see the makeup she'd used to cover the dark circles.

"What have you come up with so far?" Dash leaned forward in his chair.

"Nothing." She took a sip of her foamy cold brew. "At least, nothing you don't already know."

"Has she been distant with you lately?" he asked. "Keeping to herself?"

"A little, I guess. Why do you ask?"

"Her boss mentioned she's been keeping to herself more than usual and working from home," he explained.

"I mean, yes, but it's understandable, given the breakup."

"What breakup?" he asked.

"You don't know?" Her question shouldn't have caused another stab of guilt to pierce his chest. The sense of dread that came with feeling like he'd neglected Layla could be crushing. He should be a better brother. He should be closer to his sister so he could watch out for her.

A host of excuses came to mind, but the biggest one was the number of hours he spent working. His dedication might make him one of the best at his job, but what did that really mean when it caused him to neglect the promise he'd made on his father's grave?

Dash frowned and slowly shook his head. "Afraid not."

"Layla got her heart bruised in a new relationship." Suddenly, the rim of Raina's coffee cup became fascinating. Her inability to look him in the eye while she explained something he should already know about his sister wasn't helping ease his guilt.

He smacked the flat of his palm on the tabletop.

"Sorry," she said, low and under her breath.

"Not your fault," he ground out.

"Still…" She started to say something but stopped.

"Go on," he urged.

"No." She shook her head. Her jaw was set and her chin jutted out just a little bit. He'd seen her look of determination before and knew it was futile to keep going.

Considering how much was left unsaid between them, he figured one more couldn't make things worse. It was obvious she cared about Layla. He loved his baby sister, even though it didn't show under the circumstances.

Raina sat with her back ramrod straight. She glanced around a couple of times, no doubt checking out the exits and not realizing she was looking for an escape. Stress lines were etched in her forehead and bracketed her full pink lips—lips he didn't need to focus on for too long.

Looking at how uncomfortable she clearly was and yet was still willing to talk to him caused him to regroup and take a different approach. "Thank you for talking to me, Raina."

"I'm not doing it for you." The term *stiff upper lip* applied here.

"I'm clear on that point. Doesn't mean I don't appreciate it anyway." He exhaled. "I should have been a better brother."

"LAYLA LOVES YOU." The reason Raina felt the need to jump to Dash's defense so quickly escaped her. She hadn't planned out those words. They sprang from her lips without regard for how eager they sounded.

"That makes me an even bigger jerk for not knowing what was going on in her life." He didn't seem ready to give himself a break. She should revel in this moment. She should be ready to declare victory or shout *ha!* Except that seeing the storm brewing behind those dark brown, thickly lashed eyes was a rare sighting.

Dashiell West never showed his hand. He'd never once come off as vulnerable or afraid, or anything less than the kind of confident that bordered on being cocky. He was never afraid to flex the fact that he was damn good at his job. Life seemed to come easy to him. *Effortless* came to mind when she thought about him. Was it fair? No. There had to be more brimming under the surface considering his parents' deaths and the fact he had to raise his sister. And yet she'd never seen a single crack in his facade.

So seeing him in a moment of vulnerability about Layla caused Raina to jump to his defense before she could think through what she was going to say. Since there were no do-overs, she figured she better just roll with this one. Plus, it was true: Layla lit up every time she talked about her brother.

"What's the bastard's name?" Dash had been studying the contents of his cup. Without looking at her, he picked up his drink and took another sip. He set the cup down with purpose and then crossed his arms. The white cotton material of his shirt stretched over a broad chest with muscles stacked for days.

"I wouldn't tell you if I knew." Lying to him was harder than she expected, and she feared she would give herself away. In his present state, giving him a name would do more harm than good. Raina forced her gaze away from his hot bod. She didn't need to be reminded of Dash's physical perfection. The barista had practically fallen over when she caught a glimpse of him. Her face had turned a shade of red that was brighter than a heating element. In fact, Raina was certain she could have boiled water on it.

The second mistake she made was looking up when he didn't respond. Gaze narrowed, lips thinned—he had a murderous glare. She pitied the man who hurt Layla and wouldn't want to be on the other end of that look.

"I swear." She put her hands up, palms out, in the surrender position.

"Can you find out? My sister sure as hell won't tell me." Dash rarely swore. The fact that he'd done so twice already was another red flag. Even she knew that a good investigator had to remain objective. Could he?

"That's between you and Layla." She wouldn't touch that subject with a ten-foot pole.

"I would have known if I'd been around more." The storm brewing behind his eyes intensified. The guilt he had over his perceived shortcomings as a brother was reeling her in. His gorgeous face and worried heart were weakening resolves in her that needed to be stronger than ever. Letting her guard down for a second could end in disaster. *Already has*, an annoying voice in the back of her mind pointed out. She'd lowered her defenses once at his sister's party—and made the walk of shame the following morning after staying the night together in the guest room.

Embarrassment at the memory heated her cheeks. She should be relieved he'd told her there was no chance their fling could go any further. After her father's dangerous job left her mother a young widow, Raina had sworn off making the same mistake.

She cleared her throat and redirected. "Besides, her love life isn't what we came here to talk about."

Her bad on the word choice *love life*. The storm raged for a hot second.

Raina took in a deep breath and searched for better words.

"Will you come on board? Help with the investigation?" he asked, coming right out with the request.

"I already am, so—"

"Not from afar. I'd like to work together. Go back to my place and start hashing this out. You know my sister even better than I do. If we work together and combine our knowledge, we'll get much further."

Agreeing to his request would put her at risk. Being seen with the defendant's brother and skipping out on work weren't exactly pegs to climb on the corporate ladder. "I could lose my job if the company found out."

"I don't want that to happen. Can you take a couple of personal days? Call in sick without jeopardizing your career?" He shifted in his seat. The normally calm, cool and collected Dash was clearly on edge. The man had made it clear he didn't do… what had he called them?…*loose ends*. Or was it *frayed edges*? But he was all in when it came to his sister. She would laugh at the irony that his one "frayed edge" was a blood relative if Layla wasn't in so much trouble.

"Maybe." She shrugged. Either way, she had every plan to work on the case.

The way he studied her said he realized this. "We'll cover a lot more ground if we team up."

"You and the word *team* in the same sentence don't exactly inspire confidence." Her retort was meant to come out sassy. Instead, it sounded pathetic more than anything else. She didn't want to give away her hand and let him know that her feelings were still hurt from the way he'd left things. She also didn't want to seem like she was still pining for him either.

She wasn't. No matter how attractive he looked in that button-down shirt or how much the two day–old scruff added to his billboard-model looks. He had one of those chiseled jawlines that made facial hair actually look good. She wasn't normally big on it. The news flash that Dash was ridiculously good looking wasn't exactly a scoop.

"Please." The sincerity in his eyes was only matched by the candor in his voice—a voice that had a habit of washing over her and through her, causing a thousand goose bumps to dot her skin.

"You make a good point about getting further in the case if we pool our resources." She issued a sharp sigh and then made eye contact. Big mistake. Looking into those espresso-colored eyes sent a ripple of awareness traveling through her.

Most would make a remark at this point. Go in for the close while she waffled. Not Dash. He was *that* good. He was *that* patient.

Those terms were good descriptors of him in bed too. Maybe *mind-blowing* was better.

Raina was probably going to regret this, but all she could think about was getting Layla out of that Popsicle-orange jumpsuit and back home where she belonged.

"I'll do it." She held a finger up before he could respond. "One condition."

Rather than rush to answer, he studied her. The heat from his stare sent more of that warmth through her. He took his time before opening his mouth.

"Name it," he finally said, without breaking eye contact.

"No sex."

"I'm not going to hit on you, if that's what you think this is about." The disappointment and finality in his tone caught her off guard. He was concerned about his family, and here she was telling him not to come on to her. Not that he would, even though she had caught his gaze lingering on her mouth earlier.

Or was she seeing what she wanted? Embarrassment heated her cheeks. She needed to get over the attraction thing no matter how strong it was. Could she?

Chapter Five

"I'll do whatever it takes to help my best friend."

"Good." Dash could keep his attraction to Raina under control. "What do you say to heading back to my place?"

"Why there?" A look passed behind her pale blue eyes that he couldn't quite get a handle on. They were like looking at the sky on a clear day. Her thick, wavy hair; thick lashes and full pink lips made for one hell of a package. But restraint wasn't normally a problem for Dash, and attractive women were a dime a dozen. Intelligent, strong-minded, beautiful women like her were the exception.

"I have a great setup and can easily log into my work account from there. It's secure and will give us access to resources we won't have otherwise." His words sounded clipped even to him. He wasn't trying to give her a hard time. His mind was still reeling from the heartbreak his sister had endured and hadn't bothered to tell him about. Relationships were complicated.

"It'll be interesting to see your place for the first

time." Her words were cold and uttered with the precision of a surgeon's blade, slicing his jugular. It was obvious Raina didn't want to be in the same room with him; Layla was lucky to have a friend who cared about her so much.

Dash had work acquaintances. Friends? Not quite. If he had time for friends, he would've had time to stay up to date on Layla's social life. More of that guilt nipped at him. He should've met the bastard who broke his baby sister's heart.

That annoying voice in the back of his mind resurfaced, reminding him that his sister had a lot of secrets. She had hidden an entire relationship from him. She had to have been close to the guy or else her heart wouldn't have been hurt.

Raina knew more than she was admitting. He could tell the moment she mentioned it by watching her body language. She immediately crossed her legs and folded her arms, closing up in every way possible, as though she was putting up a barricade to keep from giving away too much.

While he appreciated her loyalty to his sister—respected it, even—she might withhold information that could be important to the case. That was unacceptable. Pushing her now would only serve to push her away. He needed her input, and he needed her shared secrets.

The only person more stubborn than Raina was Layla. His sister would only give him what she wanted him to know. As much as he considered the two of them to be close, she'd always kept him at arm's length with very private matters.

"Is your car at the office?" he asked.

"No. I took the ferry over and then walked. I wanted to clear my head." It was still summer and sunny. The morning had been beautiful—one of those perfect late-summer days before the rain and fog hit.

"You walked over in those?" He glanced down at her high heels.

"I wore tennis shoes and took them off at my desk like I usually do." She looked at him as if he was crazy. He hadn't been around her long enough to know her habits, but this sounded like something Layla would do. The similarities to his sister stopped right there.

"Then we can take my car. I'll pull around up front if you're afraid to be seen walking away with me." Protecting her job was key.

"That's probably a good idea, Dash." She exhaled when she said his name, and he didn't hate the sound of it on her lips.

"I'll text when I'm out front."

She reached across the table and touched his forearm. Electricity shot through him at the point of contact, sending currents along his skin. The way she pulled her hand back told him she'd felt it too.

"Thank you for thinking about protecting my job. I can't afford to lose it, especially under suspicious circumstances. I don't have to tell you how small the tech community can be at times." Those big eyes blinked up at him. He ignored the squeeze in his chest.

"If you get fired for helping a federal investigator, we'll go after them in court." He ground his back teeth at the idea she could be manipulated by her employer. He'd heard about the glass ceiling and unequal pay in the corporate world when it came to women. Precisely the reason Layla had insisted on the job she had. *Money doesn't discriminate* was basically her mantra. Clients were another story, but money in and of itself saw no race, color or sex.

"We'll cross that bridge when we come to it. First things first, let's get our girl out of jail."

"I'll only be a minute." Dash pushed to standing and then walked out of the café. He surveyed the lobby of the building without drawing attention to himself. With his head down, his purposeful walk worked wonders at keeping prying eyes off him.

A suit-and-tie type sat on the edge of one of the sofas near the window, studying his cell phone like it had the numbers to a hundred-and-fifty-thousand-dollar lottery jackpot on it. Halfway across the lobby, Dash caught sight of someone familiar. Layla's boss entered the turnstile.

At Dash's height, it was difficult to hide outright, so he pivoted and made a beeline for the café. He tossed his cup in the trash on the way in and then sidestepped behind a pole. Alec's reluctance to allow Dash access to Layla's desk and files came to the forefront of his mind.

The guy was dodging something. What? His excuse had been the investment firm's clients had strict confidentiality clauses in their contracts. That wasn't the only thing bothering Dash. He thought about how Alec had seemed both upset and betrayed by Layla's arrest and clear guilt.

Alec had easily volunteered the information about Layla's so-called erratic behavior of late, despite trying to play if off as concern. Alec's act of *hating to say it, let alone think it*, was just that. Except she wouldn't be the first to snap or be lured by the easy access to big money.

Dash hoped her juvenile rap sheet didn't come into play. He could only hope the media didn't figure out her crime, because she would be deemed guilty before a trial if news got out that she'd covered up her record in order to get her current job. The fact that she had the technical ability to bury her background files—which she had done using the dark web—wouldn't exactly put her in the best light right now.

There were complications to his sister's case that cast her in a bad light. The last thing he needed was someone who had better skills than him, Raina or Layla digging into the investigation. Which reminded him, he needed to find out who Layla's attorney was going to be. He had a few names to share despite his sister telling him not to worry. What phrase had she used?

"I got this." Those words haunted him. They were the same ones she'd used right before her juvie arrest.

Safely behind the pole, Dash palmed his cell phone and turned on the camera feature. He reversed the picture, turning it into selfie mode. He edged his hand out just enough until he could see Alec and the guy in the suit. Dash snapped a couple of pictures as he studied Alec's body language. He stood there with a rigid back and shoulders. He tucked his hands inside his pocket and rocked back and forth on the balls of his feet. His posture was stiff as he brought his hands out a few seconds later, right hand going straight up to his face. It was difficult to see what he did with that hand from Dash's angle. Rub his chin or forehead? But then the hand fisted, and he tucked it back inside his pocket.

Dash activated video mode and zeroed in on the guy in the suit. He could blow up the video later and read the guy's lips.

The two wrapped up whatever they were doing together. An eager handshake was followed by Alec glancing around before leaving the way he came and going, presumably, back to his office. He made a left out the door, so he was headed toward work, at the very least. But he hadn't invited the guy upstairs.

Interesting.

RAINA TAPPED HER finger on the wooden table, waiting for Dash. She checked the time on her cell phone. He should have texted by now. What was he doing?

She drained her coffee cup, feeling a buzz from too much sugar. Or was it the fact that she'd been around Dash again? It was that same heady feeling she knew was bad for her in the long run. Sure felt good in the moment, though.

The text finally came.

I'm here.

It was about time. She stood up, tossed her garbage in the trash receptacle and made her way to the front of the building.

Dash's all-black shiny and expensive sports car got looks from even money-tainted Seattleites. Cash practically oozed down the streets thanks to a certain e-commerce company's headquarters. The headquarters of a famous coffee brand gave Seattle enough caffeine to fuel the long hours most workers spent in the office.

"Fancy ride for someone who works for the government." She slipped into the passenger seat from a door that opened up instead of out, making the vehicle look like it had wings. Turned out Dash was as fancy as his sister when it came to cars. Raina had never been a fan of sports cars. Had never gotten the appeal of feeling like she was sitting an inch from the ground. She stretched her legs out in front of her, thinking how much fun getting out of this thing in a skirt was going to be—if by *fun*, she meant like swimming with alligators fun.

"It throws people off for exactly that reason and it's a leftover from my high paying tech job era," he said. Was that defensiveness she picked up on?

"It's probably best not to announce to the world you're a special agent." She seat-belted in, and he shifted gears.

"It also has enough oomph to make it up these hills." He tapped the gas and the thing responded to his lightest touch, lurching forward. The engine roared.

Raina grabbed on to the armrest for safety, wishing there was a way to brace herself for the next couple of hours with Dash.

Within minutes, he pulled into the parking garage of his building and into the space marked for the penthouse. The penthouse. Should she really be surprised? She already had so many unanswered questions about Dash, none of which she could have asked Layla without sounding off alarm bells that said Raina was into her best friend's brother. There was no way she was giving away her attraction.

The door opened with the push of a button. She threw her legs over the side and hoped she'd be able to pull herself up. There was no graceful way to do it. As she struggled, Dash came around the side of the vehicle and offered a hand up. She took it. No choice there. As she pulled herself to standing, she realized his face was turned toward the elevators. She appreciated the gesture of him not gawking at her while she struggled or accidentally showed her panties.

"Thank you," she said as she straightened her skirt.

"Welcome," was all he said, and that deep timbre still washed over her.

She grabbed her satchel containing her laptop and handbag, and then followed him to the elevator bank.

Inside, he pressed his thumb to a pad and then pushed the button marked PH.

Words escaped her as the glass elevator zipped up to the top floor soundlessly. The doors opened to an apartment with a strong masculine vibe that was surprisingly warm and welcoming. The place had character, and the space was well defined despite being very open.

The midcentury-modern furnishings blended seamlessly with the view. The place was almost overwhelmingly beautiful. Wood, stone, leather and other fabrics gave the apartment a lived-in feel. She wondered how much this place set him back financially. His government salary might cover taxes and electricity. That was about it.

"There's so much natural light here." She took in the wall of windows. Being a corner unit, the space afforded both water and city views. "It's amazing."

"Thank you." There was more than a hint of pride in his voice.

The interior was a mix of eclectic, contemporary, rustic, vintage and midcentury styles. If she tried to pull off a look like this, her place would look like a sad garage sale.

"Almost all of the wood is reclaimed," he said as he tossed a key fob into a basket near the elevator.

She took a couple more steps inside. The living room wasn't especially large, but it had everything needed for comfort. A good-sized sofa and a weathered leather chair were nestled around a hand-carved coffee table. The wall of windows overlooking the water made the place feel so much larger than it was. There was a curved balcony outside the dining area with a panoramic coastal view, and a kitchen that was a cook's dream.

"Did you decorate this yourself?" she had to ask.

"I had help." The fact that he didn't elaborate caused her to think there was probably a woman involved. An ex?

Rather than get lost down that rabbit hole, she decided to pivot. "As far as your sister goes, do you have a suspect list?"

He shook his head and motioned toward the sofa in the living room. "Do you want water or anything before we get started?"

"No thanks." She didn't need to remind herself this wasn't a social call or a date. She moved to the sofa and pulled out her laptop. There was a C-shaped side table, made from wood, conveniently positioned next to her as she sat down. She set up her laptop there, kicked off her high heels and tucked her feet underneath her bottom.

As she booted up her system, Dash took a seat next to her. The sofa dipped underneath his weight. The man was six feet four inches of muscle. From memory, he had washboard abs and the kind of long torso that transitioned into an improbable V at the hips. He had a flat piece of tech in his hands that was larger than a tablet. He tapped on it a couple of times, and what had looked like a massive painting on the opposite wall now turned into a screen. Another couple of taps and the arm of the sofa opened and a small table came up and out, like an automated version of a first-class seat on an airplane.

Working in IT, Raina made good money. It wasn't push-a-button-open-a-table money, but she drew a nice paycheck. Why Dash would leave a life where he got paid ridiculous amounts of money for his trade to work for the government, she'd never know.

"So, you don't have a suspect list. What's your next step?" she asked.

His fingers moved across the keyboard, and something resembling a whiteboard filled the screen on the wall. Using his finger on the pad/remote, he wrote the words *Suspects*, *Motive*.

Then he pushed the table away and turned to face her. With those stormy brown eyes on her, her throat dried up. She swallowed to ease some of the dryness.

"I'm more interested in where you think I should start," he said.

Chapter Six

"I've never really liked her boss much, if I'm honest. There's something about him that makes my skin crawl more than a little bit." Raina shivered, looking like a cat had walked over her grave.

"He's not my favorite person either," Dash agreed. The fact that Raina had such a visceral response to the man caused Dash to want to look into Alec Kingsley's background even more. Easy enough to accomplish with all the resources at his fingertips. However, since Kingsley was part of an official investigation, Dash had to follow the letter of the law. Which meant he had to go slow even though his sister didn't have all day. He couldn't stand to think of her locked behind bars, no matter how much she swore Popsicle orange was her color. Her mental toughness might be the stuff of legend, but everyone had a breaking point, including Layla.

"There's a guy at her office who is super competitive with her. Every time she gets an accolade, he tries to shoot her down behind her back," Raina continued.

"Name?"

"Stuart something." She snapped her fingers like it might help her remember. "Oh, it starts with an *R*. I remember because my mind immediately went to Stuart the rat."

"Sounds like a real jerk." Hearing anyone had it out for his sister was enough to get Dash's blood boiling. He wrote on the pad with his finger, and Stuart's name came up. He split the screen and pulled up the company's website. A quick scroll of names on the Representative page revealed the last name: Ross.

"That's him." She pointed.

Dash clicked on the contact, and Stuart's information came up along with his picture. He looked smart bordering on nerdy. His face was sallow. He had black hair with loose curls on top and Coke-bottle glasses. Despite the fact that he was smiling, there wasn't much Dash liked about the guy's face.

"My initial thought for the motive in this case was greed, but revenge works too," he said.

"Kill two birds with one stone." Raina studied the picture. "At the company Christmas party last year, he tried to lick my face."

Dash couldn't believe what he was hearing. "Why does he still have a job?" More anger surfaced. Dash flexed and released his fingers, trying to work off some of the tension. Any more and he'd need a full-scale workout.

"I didn't report him." She flashed her eyes at Dash. "Before you say anything else, I was going to, but he said he'd had too much to drink and was mortified. I didn't even make it home before he started calling to apologize."

"He called your personal cell?" Dash was normally cool during an interview but talking to Raina brought out all his protective instincts.

"I guess he got it from a colleague in my department." She shrugged. "Now that I think about it, the whole ordeal threw me off, so I didn't even ask how he got my number."

"Have you seen him outside of work? At your favorite coffee shop? Hanging around your building?" he asked.

"No. No. Nothing like that. I only saw him at work. Sometimes in the parking garage when I drove in." She folded her arms across her chest like she did when she was feeling vulnerable.

Dash wrote the word *stalker* under his name anyway. "Who else?"

"Well, if we're going to go down the road of stalkers, we have to consider yours." She compressed her lips like she was stopping herself from continuing.

"Talia Herzog." Her real first name was Natalia but she'd shortened it, saying it sounded more American. Dash pulled up SecureCall, an app he had created to make face-to-face calls that couldn't be hacked into or traced. "Call Madeline."

The program pulled up the contact and initiated the call.

"Damn, you have a lot of cool tech here, Dash." The admiration in Raina's voice made him smile despite his somber mood. Then again, her presence alone had him off-balance.

"Hey, Dash." Madeline Striker could only see him on her end, so it was only fair he let her know someone else was in the room.

"I have Raina Andress here with me," he immediately stated.

"Oh. Okay. Hello, Raina."

"Hi."

He jumped right in. "We're calling about Talia. Do you have a trace on her? Any recent activity?"

"Let's see." The sound of Madeline's fingers dancing on a keyboard filled the quiet. "Ah, okay. I do see activity with her. She's been circling the office and your apartment building, careful to keep the court-ordered distance."

"Doesn't sound good," he said.

"No. No. It sure doesn't. She is definitely in play in the area, sticking mostly to Seattle and Bainbridge Island. She's on Pier 52 more than you would want her to be," Madeline informed him.

Out of the corner of his eye, he saw Raina turn toward the floor-to-ceiling windows. He could read her mind. If she could see for miles, someone else would be able to see *in* from miles away.

"Let's keep a close eye on that one," he said to Madeline.

"Will do."

He thanked her before ending the call, but he could almost see Raina's wheels turning.

"Your ex worked in IT, is that right." It was more a statement than a question, but he answered it anyway. "Yes."

"What's your story with her?" The muscles in Raina's face tensed ever so slightly when she turned toward him. His ego wanted it to be because she still had a thing for him—but the wall she'd erected between them said even if she did, it wouldn't matter.

"I had to take out a restraining order against her two years ago. She wouldn't let up," he began, not enjoying airing his dirty laundry. He reminded himself that this was for Layla, and kept going. "She's smart and a good hacker. It took some doing for me to prove she'd hacked my email and social media accounts."

"Is that the reason you no longer have a personal account?"

He nodded.

"I'd started seeing someone else, and Talia wasn't put off by that. She said I would come around to the fact she was the only one for me in a matter of time," he continued.

"Only it wasn't a suggestion, I'm guessing," she said.

"No. She flattened Emma's tires, except that we couldn't prove she was responsible. A guy came out of nowhere, following Emma."

"Did he hurt her?" she asked quickly.

"Not physically. I think she was scarred mentally by being followed and 'accidents' kept happening. One to her vehicle. Then her dog came home from doggy day care really sick. The owners couldn't explain what happened. Her identity was stolen, and someone maxed out her credit card. Untangling it all was a mess, and Emma decided I was bad luck. Talia was successful at ruining the chance of continuing the relationship."

"I thought you didn't do relationships," she quipped.

RAINA WISHED SHE could reel those words back in. Too late. They were out there.

"I never said that, exactly."

Now she really wished she could be spared the pain of embarrassment. He'd said he didn't *do* relationships. What he'd meant was that he didn't *do* relationships with *her.* The sting was worse than a sunburn. But that was another rabbit hole she had no plans to trip down.

She directed the conversation back on track. "Didn't your sister mention that your ex went after you professionally?"

"She did her best to make me look incompetent at work and was almost successful there, since I hadn't initially suspected she was behind it," he admitted.

"What happened to her? Why did she stop?"

"Prison. She was sentenced to two years but was paroled six months ago for good behavior," he said.

"And according to Madeline, she's been circling like a shark." Raina's comparison must have struck a chord.

"Talia would realize that Layla is a weak spot for me," he said. "Nothing is sacred with her. She could try to frame my sister out of revenge."

"Your sister didn't like Talia."

Dash issued a sharp breath. "That's an understatement. My sister couldn't stand Talia and made no effort to hide her feelings. Talia complained that I should cut the cord with my baby sister and stop hovering. We fought about family ties, which were important to me and not her."

"But you haven't had contact with her in two years. She got out of prison six months ago. Why wait so long to strike? Why hurt Layla now?" There had to be a reason. People didn't just come out of the woodwork. Although, Talia seemed like the type who would take her time plotting her revenge. Layla could only be the beginning. Based on what had happened to his last girlfriend, Talia had a lot more to dish out.

"No. I haven't. She hasn't been legally allowed to be around me either. So she's keeping to the shadows."

"She sounds like a real piece of work," Raina said a little too loud. The fact that he was willing to date someone like that over her sat about as well as a hot poker in her stomach.

He didn't respond.

"We have to put her on the list." She no longer wanted to talk about Talia.

He nodded solemnly.

"She's the obvious choice. Too obvious." Raina tapped her finger on her armrest.

"Tell that to Seattle PD," he quipped.

"They'll figure it out. They might have to be led to the truth, but they'll get there, if we have to drag them to it." She had no plans to let her best friend rot in prison.

With his gaze focused and lips thinned, the determined look on Dash's face said he would die before that happened. Layla was lucky to have him for a big brother.

"So, obviously, the trail leads to her even though we both know she's not guilty," Raina continued.

"Plus, the money never appeared in her accounts," Dash pointed out, despite knowing it wouldn't have.

"She told me a little bit about her past. She said it was rough for a while, but she got straightened out. If any of the information comes to light, they'll skewer her at the firm," Raina said.

"The media will hound her. Plus, Alec is already pivoting his story to save his own rear end." Dash's grip on the remote caused his knuckles to turn white.

"I have no doubt he'll start backpedaling. The company will hold him accountable if one of his employees stole two million dollars, unless he distances himself." It was disgusting but true. Alec was out for himself.

"Did my sister tell you about her juvie record?" Dash asked.

Raina nodded. "Not specifics. I just knew that she'd gone through a rough patch and came out the other side because of you."

"She said that?" He shouldn't be so surprised. To Layla, he was a saint.

"Yes," she confirmed. "As far as the case goes,

I wonder if she could have been someone's unwitting accomplice."

"My sister is too smart to hand over her passwords. She's also too suspicious of everyone she meets." It seemed to dawn on him who she was talking about when his lips thinned. "Are you talking about her ex?"

"Yes."

"His name is going to come up anyway, Raina. You might as well tell me now." He made a good point.

The thought of betraying her best friend's trust sat hard. But he was right. Calum's name would come up. Raina issued a sharp sigh. "Calum Langston is his name."

Dash's lips compressed as he shook his head. "Never heard of him."

"He's the head of her department. Alec's boss. He's also a vice president who…" She flashed her eyes at him. "You're not going to like this part."

"I don't like any of this, so you might as well go on."

"He's married. But before you make a judgment, she didn't know. She knew he *was* married, but he was supposed to be in the process of a divorce. It's the reason Layla kept him under the radar. She was waiting until the divorce was final to bring him around. And I only knew recently when I stopped by her house to find him leaving. They couldn't hide from me."

"So, he manipulated my sister and you didn't tell me this immediately?" He ground his back teeth.

"It sure felt that way, and I didn't think it was my secret to tell," she admitted. "I got a bad feeling about him, so I did a little digging into his personal life. I figured I could use it against him if the relationship went sour and he tried to blackmail Layla if she became inconvenient."

"What did you find?"

"He got his wife pregnant at the time he said they weren't together," she said.

"How did my sister react?"

"She was mortified. Embarrassed. I told her right away and hated every minute of the pain I knew I was causing her. I just couldn't let him get away with using her. She was head over heels, talking about spending time together in the mountains over Thanksgiving in his family's cabin. And I use the word *cabin* loosely. *Mansion* is more like it."

"He's the reason she was withdrawing from work," he surmised.

"Yes."

"Stealing two million dollars would be a great middle finger to a man who was using her," he stated, with the kind of dread in his voice that said he thought he might be right.

"She didn't do it, though." Raina had to be clear on that point. "There were other, better ways to stick it to someone. And to be clear, she was mortified when she found out she was a mistress."

"My sister has done a lot of things in the past, but

knowingly spending time with a married man is a line she wouldn't cross," he agreed.

"Not only did she feel burned and humiliated, she felt shame. Shame that took her back to the mistakes she made in her youth. She spiraled and didn't want to face him or anyone else at the office, figuring it was only a matter of time before others found out and she was labeled. She didn't have the confidence to believe anyone would take her side because he's very well liked at the office. The guys want to be him and the women all wish they could have five minutes alone with him, no wives or husbands. He's *that* charming."

Chapter Seven

Dash wouldn't mind five minutes alone in a room with Calum Langston, but lust had nothing to do with it. He had plans to speak to this guy face-to-face and a strong desire to set the man straight that Dash knew better than to act on during an investigation. There was another question on the tip of his tongue that he had no right to ask Raina: Was Calum Langston tempting to her?

He made note of the name and moved on. There were five names on the screen: Alec. Calum. Stuart. Talia. Layla. "This gives me a place to start."

"I think we both know there are only four real suspects," she quickly pointed out. She pulled her laptop over and started tapping on the keys. "I'm shooting my boss a note to let him know that I'm working from home for the foreseeable future."

"I need a list of all my sister's acquaintances. Places she visits. Does she have a regular person at the nail salon? What about hair?"

"I have all those contacts." She grabbed her cell phone and started sharing straight to his phone. "But

I'm her best friend. Other than her relationship with Calum, I'm it. She's not the kind of person who collects a lot of friends for the sake of filling contacts on her phone. You know?"

He did know. But he should have known her better. The affair had caught him completely by surprise. There was no need to ask Raina for Calum Langston's phone number. His contact information would be on the company's website.

"Make yourself comfortable," he said to her as he stood.

"Where are you going?" One of her eyebrows shot up.

He held out his phone. "To talk to a hairdresser and nail tech." Most people spilled secrets in those places. His sister was usually the exception, but her lack of office comradery made her a good target for an older man looking for a mistress.

"I'm going with you," Raina said.

"Not this time. I'll come back and pick you up," he said.

"I could be helpful," she argued.

"And I work best alone when interviewing someone. I usually get more out of people that way." He wasn't trying to be a jerk. This was just how he preferred to work a case. "I'll swing by and pick you up before heading to prison to visit Layla."

Raina didn't seem thrilled with the plan, but she nodded.

"Stay at that. You'll do the most good on that keyboard. If we can get an IP address, we can nail the bastard." Most people were savvy enough to use a virtual private network, VPN, to deflect their signal to a place like Canada.

"I'm on it," she said, looking a little too right getting comfortable on his couch. She tucked a throw pillow behind her back and settled in. "I wish I'd brought yoga pants and a T-shirt, though."

"Any preference for lunch?" He could pick up something on the way back. Cooking was not in his skill set. Heating and reheating were more up his alley. He had a steady supply of what he called "divorced-man meals" delivered from one of those services. The food was edible. He got by on it. But it was nothing to write home about.

"Tacos sound good."

He liked that she ate real food with him. Salads were for rabbits, not people. Then again, he couldn't see his sister hanging around with someone who wouldn't go for the occasional burger. Layla knew how to eat. Preparing food wasn't a West family forte, despite the fact that their father could throw down a steak on a grill like nobody's business. Their mother's cooking could best be described as *edible, but with a good effort.* Or maybe, made with love. He hadn't thought about his parents in a long time, and he never talked about them. An all-too-familiar pain stabbed him in the chest.

"Easy enough." He checked the time. There was a taco shop on the corner. But the food truck was even better. Before he headed out, he remembered the suit and tie from earlier who'd met with Alec.

Dash brought up the video on his cell phone. He froze the frame on a clear shot. "Have you ever seen this guy before?"

She studied the screen and then shrugged. "No idea who he is."

"Any chance he works at the firm?" he asked.

"I don't recall seeing him before. The suit is expensive. Looks handmade." He had thought the same thing. "Most client meetings happen in our building. We have some pretty elaborate conference rooms with snacks and drinks. There's no reason to leave the building to get coffee. When we have big client meetings, everything is catered."

Most people who worked in the IT field wore jeans and a relaxed shirt, but the fact that Raina wore a skirt and blouse meant everyone had to look their best. And she looked damn good in that form-fitting skirt.

He could bring the video up on the big screen later. Right now, he needed to visit the beauty industry and then grab some tacos.

"I'll be back." He pocketed his cell phone and grabbed his key fob from the bowl. The only other woman who had been to his apartment at all was Layla, not even Talia or Emma.

Dash decided not to read too much into it. Raina was there to work on a case, and having her at his home kept her in his sight.

On the elevator, he checked both contacts, nail and hair. He determined which was farthest—hair— and decided to hit that one first. Layla's hairstylist was named Rikki. No last name. Just Rikki. *This should be interesting.*

Distracted, he didn't realize the elevator had reached the garage until the doors opened. He walked over to his sports car, thinking he needed to take the Lexus out next time with Raina. He'd seen her struggle to get in and out of his sports car, which was too low to the ground for someone wearing a skirt.

The drive to Layla's hairdresser took half an hour in traffic. The salon was one of those individual suite–type places. Rikki occupied number seven. That was Layla's lucky number, Dash thought. Or at least it had been when she was a kid. Was it still? There was too much he didn't know about his baby sister.

But Rikki's place suited her. This came as no surprise. The building was nondescript on the outside, in a typical newly built strip center. But inside, there were chandeliers and fluffy white rugs everywhere. The exposed piping that had been painted black was meant to give the place an industrial-chic look. The gray walls and black trim added to the ambience and opulence.

"Can I help you, sweetheart?" The man who greeted him was three inches shorter than Dash and had almost as much facial hair. He had on a full face of flawless makeup and he would be considered attractive in a made-up sense. His hair was platinum blond, long and had been straightened.

"Are you Rikki?" he asked, just to confirm what he already knew.

"Depends on who's asking." Rikki looked Dash up and down, sizing him up. His gaze lingered on the weapon in his holster.

"Dash West. I'm Layla's brother."

"Oh." Rikki straightened up, and he gained another inch in height. "Ohmygod. Honey…" He dropped his gaze to his client, who was staring at Dash through the mirror. "Hold tight. I'll be right back, sugar."

Rikki almost flew out of his suite. "Follow me."

They wound down a long hallway and circled around to the back suites. On the right, there was a small break room with the door propped open. Rikki motioned for Dash to follow him inside and then he kicked the stopper out of the way. The door closed with an audible thump, and Rikki whirled around.

"How is our girl?" he asked, concern knitting his eyebrows together.

"You know Layla. She says she's fine."

"How could she be? The food must be horrendous in a place like that." Rikki seemed horrified.

Prison wasn't known for gourmet cooking. No Michelin-starred restaurants in lockup.

"Wait, that was a stupid thing to say. The food is the least of her problems," Rikki said.

"I'm talking to her friends. Seeing if I can piece together how any of this could have happened." He didn't say 'on my watch' despite thinking it.

"Of course you are. You're an amazing brother.

Lay—" he flashed his thick-lashed eyes at Dash "—that's what I call her."

Dash nodded his understanding.

"Lay talked about you all the time," Rikki said. "Like, *all* the time."

As heart-warming as that sounded, Dash highly doubted it was true.

Rikki gave him a once-over. "What do you want to know?"

"Who her friends were. Who she talked about. Her relationship status. What was going on in her life." He figured that covered the basics.

"Okay. Here goes. She was thinking about getting a dog because she just had a rough breakup," Rikki claimed. "Boyfriend turned out to be married. She took it hard."

Nothing Dash didn't already know. Still, he nodded and played the part.

"What else? Hmm." Rikki's gaze became unfocused, like he was looking inside himself for more information. He was being honest and genuine. "She'd been working from home a lot lately." He perked up. "Oh. And the last time she was here, she seemed super paranoid. Like she half expected the guy's wife to show up or something. I asked her about it, but she shrugged it off. You know Lay. When she doesn't want to share, she doesn't talk."

Dash had planned on investigating Calum and his wife. This news bumped them both up the list. "Did she mention any names?"

Rikki shook his head. "Never. She just called him 'VP.'"

"Did she mention spending time with anyone else recently?" Dash asked.

"Not that I can think of," Rikki said. "Not lately. She just acted paranoid when she was here. And she got right in and out, which wasn't like her. Then she canceled her last two appointments before…"

Rikki gave him another look as though he couldn't speak the words out loud. He teared up.

"Did anyone ever come in with her?" Dash asked.

"No." Rikki shivered like the question offended him. "Why would they?"

"I have no idea. I'm just throwing spaghetti against the wall, so to speak."

"I gotcha." Rikki exhaled. "This whole thing is so not cool."

He could say that again.

"That's as much as I know. Lay kept her secrets," Rikki said.

Dash thanked Rikki for his time and then exited the maze-like building. It would be just like his sister to come to a place that had privacy instead of those open-air buffet-style chop shops where conversation hummed and hairdressers stood within a few feet of each other.

His visit to an older woman who went by the name of Hun—presumably meant to be Hon—at the sleek nail salon Layla frequented went the same way as his meeting with Rikki.

Layla had been nervous about something or someone. Was she being stalked? Or afraid of getting busted?

RAINA REFUSED TO let frustration get the best of her as
she typed a little faster this time. It wouldn't help, but
it made her feel like she was doing something. She
stared at the screen mounted on the wall with suspect
names. Her stomach reminded her lunch had come
and gone. She ignored the pangs, thinking about the
word *motive* instead. What motivation would someone have to set Layla up?

With the kind of program the hacker had used, it
could be random. It probably didn't feel that way to
Layla right now, but hackers broke into systems all
the time just because they could. Virus-protection
software? She almost laughed out loud. Those had to
be right up there with the number one reason someone's system was breached. They had more back
doors than a hotel.

Speaking of snooping around, the temptation to
go through Dash's personal things was ever present.
She tried to convince herself that she wanted to get
to know him better. That it would somehow kill the
attraction simmering between them. But she managed to keep the urge in check. It would be an inva-
sion of his personal space. She could hunt around in
people's computers with her skill set, but her code
of ethics wouldn't allow for it. Rummaging through
his kitchen drawers was no different.

So, back to motive and Layla's case. There was
the obvious reason…greed. Two million dollars was

a lot of money. Layla had money in the bank. She made plenty to live a nicer lifestyle than Raina. Was it enough?

Despite trying to be objective, Raina was going to fall short. She couldn't imagine Layla ruining what she had worked hard for over a couple million dollars. If she kept at her job and continued doing as well as she had been, she'd make that in a few years.

Of course, setting her up would be one heck of a way to get her fired and discredited. She wouldn't be able to take her talents to another firm with a criminal record. Not to mention the humiliation she was suffering.

Raina's mind snapped to Calum. Was he that callous? Calculating? He hadn't become vice president for lack of political skills. Those jobs were hard to get, and one had to play their cards just right to snag a promotion like that. Also noted was the fact that he was probably one of the youngest VPs—if not *the* youngest—in the company's history.

Calum was climbing the ladder. Maybe, out of hurt, Layla had threatened to expose their relationship when she found out about the pregnancy. Layla had a temper. Not a fly-off-the-handle or say-something-she-regretted-in-the-moment kind of temper, but the slow, seething type. She definitely would have fired back at him.

Had she threatened to expose their relationship? With her skills, she could have hacked into his computer system and found all kinds of dirt on him.

Calum was a definite possibility. So was his wife.

What about Stuart? He was certainly a creep. Her skin crawled just thinking about him. He'd had a thing for Raina and—she was pretty certain—one for Layla too. He was nerdy and she never really trusted him. Knowing Layla, she would have put him in his place if he hit on her.

That could be enough for a guy like him to target her. She made a note to ask Dash if they could swing by Stuart's house after he got off work. She didn't know Dash's habits, but Layla would. Speaking of Layla, Raina needed to see that her friend was okay with her own two eyes.

The elevator doors opened and interrupted her thoughts. Dash walked into the room, wearing a frown.

"What's wrong?" she asked, sitting straight up, thinking it felt a little too right to be here.

"We have a name to add to the list."

Chapter Eight

Dash set the box of tacos down on the table and then walked over to the sofa and sat on the edge. He was too antsy to commit to the seat, and they weren't sticking around for long anyway. "Have you ever met Calum's wife?"

Her sky-blue eyes bright, Raina perked up at his question. "Yeah, sure. I mean, I'm sure I have at some point. She would have been at Christmas parties. But, no, I don't know her personally."

"Rikki said Layla was paranoid and that she skipped her last couple of appointments." He filled her in on the conversation he'd had with Rikki and the similar one he'd had with Hun roughly twenty minutes later.

"'Paranoid'?" Raina blinked at him. "I guess I never picked up on that. But then, honestly, I've had to practically force myself on her lately. Before she ended the relationship with Calum, she was with him more than not, so I gave her space."

"It shouldn't be too difficult to find out his wife's first name," he said.

"While we're on the subject of suspects, I'd like to swing by Stuart's place after we visit Layla. See how he reacts after everything that's happened." She stood. "Right now, I'm starving."

"Tacos are on the table." He was pointing out the obvious.

She took in a deep breath. "They smell amazing."

Dash walked over to the table with her, taking his gaze off her sweet, round bottom. He'd lost his appetite after talking to Rikki. Forcing himself, he managed to take down a six-pack of tacos.

"Mmm. These are the best. Where did you get them?" she asked, and he tried not to let the purr of appreciation distract him.

"Taco truck."

"I would have known if I'd had one of these before." She polished off her fourth, and he liked how she felt comfortable enough around him to really eat.

"Ready?" Raina was studying him.

He'd been so lost in thought he hadn't noticed she was done eating. "Almost. I just want to check one thing before we leave."

He palmed his cell phone and walked over to the setup in his living room. He tapped the screen a couple of times, bringing up the video of Alec and the suit onto the TV. He grabbed the remote and slowed the video to a crawl so he could watch the suit's lips move, see if he could catch what he said.

Dash intensified his gaze on the screen and replayed the video a few times. The suit's head was tilted just enough to make it next to impossible to read his lips. That was unfortunate. Dash pulled up the program he'd written for just such an occasion and launched it. He fixed the video on a play loop, set down the remote and walked over to the elevator.

"Let's go see Layla, then Stuart," he said.

"Did you figure out what he was saying?" Raina's head was cocked to one side.

"Not yet." Dash held his hand out for Raina to go first.

She collected her purse and then entered the elevator. The ride down was quick. Despite living on the top floor, the elevator was rigged not to stop off at any of the other floors if the penthouse button had been pushed, and vice versa. It came in handy and was one of the many reasons he'd bought the apartment in this building. The reno job it had required was extensive. He'd hired the best, and the end result was better than he could've hoped for. Lately, though, he was restless there. Was it time to move on? Find a new project to tackle? A new reno to get lost in? He needed some kind of change in his life. Was a change of address enough?

Raina started toward the sports car, but he grabbed on to her elbow to guide her in the opposite direction.

"I thought we were driving," she said.

"We're taking the sport utility." He pointed to the black-on-black Lexus.

"Oh. Nice."

"I thought it might be easier for you to get in and out of, considering what you're wearing," he explained, ignoring the jolt of electricity from their contact.

"That's really considerate of you, Dash." He didn't want to like how his name sounded rolling off her tongue.

Rather than respond, he walked her to the passenger side and opened the door for her.

"That's not necessary," she said quickly. "This is not a date."

"Common courtesy," he mumbled, wondering why it felt like he'd just taken a hit. The situation with his sister had him off-kilter. That was the only explanation for how drawn he felt to Raina. Don't get him wrong, she was a beautiful woman. She was wicked smart. She could be funny and charming. Don't even get him started on those sky-blue eyes of hers. He could look into them for hours.

He walked over to the driver's side and claimed his seat, then zipped out of the parking lot and onto the road headed toward Seattle Women's Correctional Facility, where Layla was being held.

"When was the last time you spoke to her?" Raina asked.

"She won't speak to me," he said. "But she will now."

"What makes you so sure?"

"First off, I have you this time. Secondly, I already know what she didn't want to tell me herself. Now that I know about Calum, she won't refuse to see me." He was confident in that fact. But just in case, he had Raina.

"What makes you believe she'll see me?" she asked.

"You're her best friend. She's been locked up for a week, with no one to speak to but her lawyer. I'm guessing she has a lawyer. She refused the one I sent," he admitted.

"Your sister can dig her heels in when she doesn't want to do something," Raina said.

"That's putting it lightly." At least he understood why she'd refused his visits. She was embarrassed about the affair. She had done the same thing after being sent to juvie. Eventually, he got it out of her that she wanted to pull the plug on their relationship because in some ways he reminded her of their father, a cop, who was good through and through.

Layla's young mind had decided she wasn't worthy of love after some of the things she'd done.

Using voice tech, Dash sent a text to Madeline requesting she find out the name of Calum Langston's wife and any other details about the woman in question. What sorority did she pledge? Where did she volunteer? What college did she go to? What kind of degree did she have? What were her technical skills? Who were her friends? Where did she live? More of those questions came, followed by the one Dash wasn't certain he wanted the answer to, which was how many children did the couple have?

He owed it to the team to bring them up to date about his visit with Rikki, and yet his protective instincts for his sister caused him to hold back. He'd brief them at the end of the day, after the visit with

Layla. She had to know that news of the affair would get out, making her look that much more guilty. He could see the headline now: "Scorned by Company VP, an Underling Gets the Ultimate Revenge." another nail in Layla's coffin. He also requested the dirt on Calum Langston.

Madeline's response was immediate. "On it."

RAINA SAT QUIETLY, listening and letting her own thoughts wander. The fact that Calum could deny Layla had been the one to sever romantic ties and it would be her word against his burned Raina up. She could see his response playing out. He'd made a mistake, he would say. He'd had an affair with a temptress in his office. Someone who practically threw herself at him. If Layla's background came to light, public opinion would be with Calum despite the truth.

He could plead for sympathy, say his wife forgave him when he asked and play the whole we're-starting-a-family-together card. He'd be forgiven. Layla would be skewered. She would lose her job and her reputation would be damaged beyond repair. The whole situation frustrated Raina. Despite all the strides that had been made in recent years in situations where men used their power to get women to sleep with them, Layla's past would always haunt her.

Plus, she'd had an affair with him willingly. He would be smart enough not to leave a trail—no text messages pleading for her to meet him. Dash would check into those just to make sure, but she doubted he'd find what they were looking for.

Rikki's and Hun's revelations had Raina's mind reeling. Layla hadn't mentioned anything about being afraid. So that was news to Raina. It seemed her best friend had kept secrets, which was another reason for the public not to trust her. Would a court of law see through all the messiness to the real Layla?

SeaTac, also known as the Federal Detention Center, was a prison operated by the Federal Bureau of Prisons. It was located in SeaTac, Washington—thus the name—near the Seattle-Tacoma International Airport, twelve miles south of downtown Seattle. The facility housed inmates as well as those awaiting trial and other people Raina didn't want her best friend anywhere near.

She reminded herself Layla was strong and had survived being in juvie. She would know how to handle herself in any situation, including this one. And yet fear for her friend's well-being kicked Raina's imagination into high gear. Layla had cleaned up her act. She wasn't the same person who'd spent time in juvie. Plus, that was a long time ago.

Layla was used to the finer things in life now. She had a nice apartment. Granted, it wasn't quite as nice as Dash's, but he had almost a decade head start. Other than his cars and penthouse, he lived a low-key life. Given a chance, Layla would surpass him.

Driving up to the nondescript white building made of sharp angles and very few windows made this nightmare a little too real. Dash parked and then came around to her side. Before he could get there, she opened her door and exited the vehicle. There was no way she was confusing this for a date for obvious reasons, but there was no reason to blur the line. Their alliance was temporary and for Layla's benefit only.

Raina needed to remind herself of that fact because being with Dash felt like the most normal thing, even when her stomach free-fell and electricity jolted through her every time they had incidental contact.

If Dash was put off by her getting out of the vehicle before he opened her door, he covered it well. In fact, his face was unreadable, and she figured that made him very good at his job when he had to interview someone.

She walked beside him and gripped her purse strap so tight her knuckles turned white. Taking in a slow breath to calm her rattled nerves, she walked first into the lobby, where they were greeted by a detention officer and then taken to a visitor's cell.

It was surreal to think she was here, visiting her friend. Even crazier that Dash was sitting beside her.

His back teeth were clenched so tight she feared he might crack a tooth. For all his smooth veneer, he was as stressed as she was about the visit.

After twenty minutes, Raina spoke up. "Does this mean she is refusing to see us?"

"Your guess is as good as mine," he admitted. "I can pull a few strings, but she won't be happy about it."

"No, she won't."

"I guess it's time to see just how angry she can get." He started to get up when the adjacent door opened.

Dash sat back down fast. He glanced at Raina, and her heart did that free fall thing again. But she couldn't focus on him right now. Instead, she watched as her best friend was walked into the room, hands cuffed in front of her.

"Layla," Raina said under her breath. The shock of seeing her best friend in an awful orange-colored jumpsuit would stick in Raina's mind for a long time to come.

Layla's gaze narrowed as she locked in on her brother. "You shouldn't have come."

"Well, I'm here now, so why don't you take a seat so we can clear the air." His voice was a study in calm.

Hands clasped, Layla didn't so much as give the slightest glance at Raina.

"Are you staying or going, Ms. West?" the guard asked.

For a hot second, Raina expected Layla to tell him she was leaving. And then she exhaled.

"I'm okay," she said.

"You know the rules. You have to take a seat." The guard looked to be in his late forties if he was a day. He had a bulbous nose and a face scarred from acne.

"Fine. I'll sit." She did, scooting the seat across from her brother.

The guard nodded, chained her to the desk and

then stood sentinel next to the door leading back from where she came. The way he stood there reminded her of a Buckingham Palace guard. Eyes forward, back erect. He certainly looked the part except for the general lack of color of his uniform.

Layla's, on the other hand, was so bright Raina could use a pair of sunglasses.

"What do you want to talk about?" Layla fixed her gaze on her brother like she was daring him to speak the awful truth out loud. She was an inmate. She'd messed up big time. This was a side to Layla that Raina had never seen before.

Chapter Nine

Instead of taking the bait, Dash raked his fingers through his hair. "We're working on getting you out of here."

"No one is going to believe I'm innocent." Layla had gone into self-preservation mode, just like she had when he'd visited her in juvie.

"But you are, and we're going to prove it." Dash left no room for doubt in his voice.

"Whatever. I have my own plan," she retorted.

"My team needs your passwords in order—"

Layla was shaking her head before he could finish.

"It's the best way to help you," he said.

"Fine." She rattled off a few faster than Dash could memorize them.

"Slower this time, Layla," he said.

She complied but not without an attitude.

"Why did you bring her?" There was a crack in Layla's tough exterior despite how quickly she recovered.

"I asked to come," Raina said. "Your brother just gave me a ride over."

"You shouldn't be in a place like this. It's not safe." Layla's chin quivered. Her tough-girl routine was dissipating faster than fog when the sun came out.

"Layla. I'm here for you. I care about you. Besides, I have your brother to watch out for me. You're the one who is—"

"No, I'm fine." She might tell herself that a hundred times, but Dash could see it in her brown eyes. His sister was definitely not okay.

"Who did it?" he came right out and asked. She had to have her suspicions.

"Short answer?"

He nodded.

"I don't know."

When he didn't respond, she added, "All I do know is that someone has been following me for a couple of weeks."

"Like a private investigator?" he asked.

"Or hit man," she said a little too quickly. Her fast response gave him the impression she was being completely honest. She glanced around like she didn't want the guard to hear her, and he realized part of her initial tough-guy act was probably to maintain some credibility inside.

Dash balled his hands into fists at the thought that he was going to get up and walk out of here without her when their time was up.

"You've already been set up for embezzlement. You're the one in federal prison." The last time he sat across a table like this from her, she'd seemed so small and vulnerable. Angry too. The anger had come across immediately. The hard outer shell had come out, making him wonder if there would be anything salvageable in there after talking to her.

Now? She was a grown woman. Still angry. But capable and smart. Also savvy.

"You need a good lawyer. I have names," he started, but she was shaking her head.

"I hired one," she said.

"Who?"

"Edward McConnell," she supplied.

"How are you paying him?" Her assets would be frozen, pending a full investigation.

"He owes me a favor," she said.

"He's connected, Layla. Hiring him makes you look guilty." McConnell handled high profile cases involving wealthy—and very guilty—people.

"Everyone already thinks I'm guilty, Dash. In case you hadn't noticed." She tried to throw her hands up in the air but was stopped by the chains. The clack sound echoed across the room.

"I don't," Raina spoke up.

Layla exhaled and it was like a balloon deflated in her chest. "You're my best friend. No one is going to believe you. Plus, you should distance yourself from me, Raina. You'll lose your job."

"I don't care," came Raina's response.

"I do. I won't be responsible for ruining two lives."

"I'm a big girl, Layla. I'm fully capable of ruining my own life. I don't need you for that." Raina's attempt to lighten the mood fell flat.

"We both know you need that job. Plus, you won't get a reference if they think you're still hanging out with me. Listen carefully. This is what I want you to do." Layla leaned in. "Go back to work and pretend like I never existed. No one has seen us together lately. Tell them you found out about—" she flashed her eyes "—and demanded that I break it off. When I didn't, you cut me out of your life."

Raina was already shaking her head. "I won't do it, Layla. Forget the idea."

"Your mom's care isn't cheap, Raina. Think about what you're doing."

"I'll figure it out." Raina's cheeks flushed like she was embarrassed. "I always do. Besides, they can't fire me."

Obviously, there was more to the story. There was also no way Dash was going to allow Raina's career to be ruined over this investigation. He made a mental note to ask about her mother later.

"Let's just say for argument's sake that Raina isn't going anywhere," Dash interrupted.

Layla blew out a sharp breath but didn't speak.

"Tell me about your relationship with Calum Langston," he said.

Layla's eyes widened in a moment of shock. Her mouth formed the word 'how' despite no sound coming out.

And then it seemed to dawn on her that he was good at his job.

"Of course you would figure it out," she said low and under her breath.

She exhaled before launching into the story of their relationship. She explained the situation in a similar fashion to Raina. Essentially, he was a jerk who was using her to have an affair. Dash could wait for Madeline's response to get answers to some of the more sensitive questions, so he didn't waste time putting Layla on the spot.

"Why would he set you up?" he asked directly.

"You're asking me?" She smacked the flat of her palm against the sterile white table between them. "Because he's a jerk who didn't want to get caught with his hand in the cookie jar?"

Dash didn't care for the reference when it came to his little sister, but he overlooked it for the sake of time.

"Why would sending you to prison be good for him?" he asked.

"I'm guessing he discredited me so his wife wouldn't believe a word I said. I stupidly threatened to tell her all about us."

He had to ask. "Were you going to?"

"No. I was angry at him. He lied to me and made me a mistress." She cast her eyes down.

"Don't do that. Don't blame yourself. Anyone can be tricked when they're in love."

"Is that what happened with you and Talia?" Layla lashed out when she couldn't deal with her emotions. Bringing up his ex was a tactic to get him off his game so he wouldn't notice how much she was hurting.

"Maybe. What does it matter now?" Except that Talia had returned and could be responsible for targeting Layla. She needed to know. "Talia's back, by the way."

For a split second, he thought her jaw might hit the floor. "When did she get out?"

"Six months ago. You should know that she's been around my work and my apartment. I had no idea until earlier today," he admitted.

"That's not good news. The woman is not well."

"That may be true, but she's also a threat. She has the kind of skills to pull something like this off," he said. He took note that Raina had gotten quiet.

"So, my brother's ex-lover is coming after me?"

Raina crossed her arms over her chest and rubbed her elbows, like she was staving off the cold. The temperature in the room hovered on the warm side, so it couldn't be from that.

"It's a possibility," he said. "One that we can't afford to ignore."

Layla's brain started churning. She was being abrupt and more than a little obnoxious, which told him she had all her defenses going at the moment. Defenses that would allow her to turn around and be taken back into a cell by the guard standing at the door. So he would cut her some slack.

"I'll keep that in mind," she finally said, but he could almost see the shift in direction happening in her mind.

"Five more minutes, Ms. West," the guard said with a finality that said there was no give-and-take.

Layla leaned back in her chair. Her gaze shifted to Raina. "I'm embarrassed you have to see me like this."

"Don't be. I know you didn't do it. I know the truth about Calum, and I'll make certain—"

"No," Layla interrupted. "You won't. Think about it, Rain. If Calum is responsible and he did this to me, he'll have no problem taking you down. Don't risk it, okay?" Layla's shoulders sagged. "It's bad enough that I'm in here. I can't have you in the cell next to me."

Dash's stomach clenched. "She won't be. Not on my watch."

"Okay. Good. Now get out of here before they kick you out." Layla was taking charge of the situation, trying to decide when they left rather than have the time forced on her. It was a defense mechanism to give her some semblance of control, so he didn't fight it.

Instead, he stood up. "I'll send you the name of a new lawyer."

Layla shook her head furiously. "Trust me on this one. My guy is the best."

Dash had already pointed out that the man represented criminals, not innocent people like her. But then, maybe she had her reasons. He could save the argument for another time.

Raina stood up first, and the look on her face said they were going to have words once they got back in the car.

"WHAT DID YOU mean by 'not on my watch'?" Raina didn't need Dash fighting her battles. She was capable of looking after herself.

"I'd like to swing by your place so you can pick up a couple of things that would make you more comfortable at my apartment," Dash said as he started the vehicle.

"I thought you didn't bring women home, Dash."

"I don't. And you're not a woman," he said and then seemed to hear how the words sounded as they came out of his mouth. "We both know you're a woman. You're not just *any* woman. You're important to my sister." He reached across and closed his hand around hers. "And to me."

The contact sent a jolt through her hand and up her arm. She pulled back in the same manner she would if she'd been bitten by a snake.

"Don't play that card with me, Dash." She had no intention of being manipulated by his charm, no matter how much her mind tried to argue he genuinely cared.

He didn't deny it, and she appreciated him for it. Instead, he issued a sharp sigh. "This is too little, too late, but I do miss you. That part is the honest truth. Also, I would say just about anything right now to reassure my sister, as long as it was legal and had a hint of truth to it. In this case, there's more than a hint. I do realize after the way we left things that I'm probably not high on your list of favorite people right now."

She folded her arms across her chest, waiting to hear the rest of what he had to say.

"Doesn't mean I don't care about what happens to you, Raina."

The reality she might be in danger started to sink in. Her association with Layla could get her in trouble with someone like Calum. Mainly, she knew the truth of what had happened between them. He could deny it all day long, but she'd been the one to figure out his wife was pregnant.

"By the way, you mentioned that you were the one who told my sister about Calum's wife. How did you find out she was pregnant?"

"Same gynecologist," she supplied. "He was there in the waiting room with his wife. They were sitting to one side of the room, so I didn't think he saw me. I could be wrong, though."

"How far along was his wife?" he asked.

"Not very. She wasn't showing or anything, but the only reason I ever see a guy at a gynecology appointment is because his wife is expecting. They always look like they feel a little out of place," she mused. "Seeing him and realizing he was in a relationship with my best friend made me curious if they were there for any other reason. So I started digging around in his inbox."

"That's illegal," he quickly countered.

"Not if you work in the tech department and find an issue on a VP's computer. I basically get free rein if he leaves his inbox up. Besides, I had to test his system." None of what she found would hold up in a court of law—even she realized that. But she was an employee doing her job. "Her pregnancy won't be easy to hide for much longer. By the time Layla goes to trial, his wife will be showing. I'd bet money on it."

"Still, any information you gained would be inadmissible."

"True. But I'm not the one on trial here. That jerk is, and his secrets will come to light very soon if he did this to Layla," she said.

"Who at work knows about me?" he asked.

"Are you asking who knows Layla's brother works for the FBI? Or are you asking if people know she has a brother?"

"There a difference?"

"Yes. A big one, at that. People know she has a brother, but she doesn't go around talking about what you do for a living. Mostly, in team-building sessions, people talk about their own career goals, life goals. I doubt anyone knows the down and dirty about your background," she said. "Except her boss, of course, since you spoke to him first thing this morning."

"Why didn't she want me to come by her office?" His question surprised her. "Was she ashamed of me in some way?"

"No." She shook her head. "Nothing like that. If anything, she was too proud of you." Raina looked him up and down. "It's just that you're...*you*."

"I'm afraid you're going to have to spell it out for me because I have no idea what that means."

"Your looks attract a lot of attention. She didn't want people gawking at you or fawning over you. She wanted to keep a professional image, plus..."

This next part was just a guess but an educated one based on several years of friendship. "People who work for the government make our higher-ups a little nervous. No one ever says it outright but, come on, a federal investigation would cripple us and make investors run. So…"

"She was afraid my job would put hers at risk," he said.

"Yes. But that didn't mean she wasn't proud of you. She practically burst with pride every time she talked to me about you."

"Speaking of you… Layla mentioned your mother," he said.

"My mom needs full-time care. I supply it." Raina sank into the passenger seat. End of story.

A decent chunk of Raina's salary went to the rehab center where her mother was currently living while relearning how to walk after a traumatic brain injury from a boating accident. What was left went to basics like rent, food and car payments. She was still paying off school loans, so there was that.

As Dash took the next hill descending toward downtown, there was a quick flash of light to her right followed by the words, "Get down."

Chapter Ten

A crotch-rocket motorcycle zipped up behind Dash's SUV. The shooter? "Keep your head down."

He sank in the seat as low as he could while still able to see over the dash. Speeding down toward the water with gunfire coming from behind wasn't exactly his favorite idea. Rather than continue down the steep incline, he took a hard left at the next intersection into oncoming traffic.

Horns blared as he navigated around the vehicles, with angry drivers flipping him the bird and waving fists at him. Crotch-rocket was still behind him. Low handlebars made for an aerodynamic ride. This bike wasn't meant for lazy Sunday cruising. It was created for speed and gave the rider the ability to zip in and out of traffic. At a hundred miles an hour without a stabilizer, the handlebars would shake and the rider could lose control if he or she so much as nipped a rock in the road. But that wouldn't be a problem on these streets, with their thirty-miles-per-hour speed limits and narrow roads.

Crotch-rocket roared up beside Dash. The rider's

face was hidden behind a helmet with a dark lens. He was male, based on his physique. Somewhere around average height and build. Lean underneath the black leather jacket he had on. He wore black jeans and boots. His boots had thick soles. He had on black gloves.

There was also a Sig Sauer in his right hand. He glanced over and extended his hand toward Dash's face.

Dash hit the brake. Hard. So hard that his head jutted forward. Crotch-rocket zipped onto the curb and slowed his pace. Glancing in the rearview—out of habit more than anything else, considering he was on a one-way street—Dash put the gearshift in reverse and mashed the gas pedal.

Before the intersection, he slowed to a crawl. Crotch-rocket adjusted to the new plan and was racing toward Dash head-on. He had no choice but to go for it and pray no one was coming.

Fortune smiled on him when he backed up. He managed to position himself in the right lane, heading up the hill and away from downtown, without hitting anyone in the process. A Porsche came close but managed to zip around him. He thought about his sports car and wished he was in it for the same reason.

"Where is he?" Raina asked, lying low on the seat.

"Coming up on your side." If Dash timed it just right, he could squeeze the motorbike against the row of parked cars coming up. He swerved toward the rider as a threat and to throw him off guard. Dash crossed over the middle of the road, netting another round of honks from oncoming traffic. At least they were driving slowly and had time to react. Nonlocal drivers always took their time going down the steep hills toward downtown. The inclines could be scary to newcomers.

The motorcycle zoomed up beside Dash's vehicle. The biker turned his gun toward the passenger window. Dash wheeled right at the exact moment a reaction from the biker would cause him to crash into another vehicle.

He did and went flying. Using voice command, Dash called 9-1-1. "Tell the operator exactly what just happened. Ask for police and ambulance. Lock the door the second I'm out."

Dash flew out of the driver's seat as the line rang for the second time. He drew his weapon and pulled his badge from the clip on his holster. Using the SUV as a barrier between him and the shooter, he moved around the front of the vehicle. He crouched to the ground, searching for signs the rider was mobile.

Rule number one in law enforcement was never run to an injured man. The flip had been spectacular, and the biker should be lying on the concrete sidewalk. It was possible he rolled over the car he'd struck. The vehicle would have taken some of the impact from the crash.

There was no sign of the guy. *Not good*, Dash thought. Was it possible he'd landed on top of a vehicle? Or crashed so hard he broke the back windshield and ended up inside the car?

The motorcycle had flipped a couple of times up-hill before momentum caught up. Then it skidded on its side to the street below. There were voices. Shouting. A scream. It all went down so fast Dash was still mentally processing.

He would have time to dissect his thoughts later. Now, he needed to find the biker. With measured steps, he inched closer to the initial spot of the crash. The sedan's emergency sirens were splitting the air.

Car by car, he moved toward the sound, his weapon leading the way.

A trail of screams sent a cold shiver racing down his spine. Dash picked up the pace as safely as he could. He reached the car. Weapon extended, he came up on the side of the white sedan.

The point of impact on the back windshield had left it looking like a spiderweb. The center of the glass was dented. There was no sign of the biker. No way could he have taken a fall like that and survived without some heavy-duty equipment. There were button-down collared shirts that could take a bullet.

Dash was confused as to how someone could walk away from an accident like this, because there was no sign of the biker anywhere. Was there someone around to clean up the mess?

He walked down to the motorcycle and snapped a couple of pics. No license plate, but he wasn't surprised.

More sirens joined the sedan's. Dash checked on his SUV. Raina looked to be fine in there. Thankfully, she stayed put and was most likely in shock.

He needed to get back to her but he waved down the first marked car he saw. Badge in hand, he returned his firearm to his holster.

He surveyed the area. The few people had scattered. This area was residential on top of businesses. Employees started filing out onto the sidewalk, questions written all over their faces as they looked toward the sources of the noise. It was probably too much to hope someone had seen something that could be useful.

But then what would it have been? It was impossible to get a description of the biker. Dash glanced around at the mixed-use buildings. Did he have help? A network would make sense. It would explain how the guy seemed to have disappeared.

An officer pulled up next to the motorcycle just as Dash was thinking they might be able to get some DNA off the bike or the busted windshield. He needed to get back to check on Raina. For now, he put his hands in the air, badge in his right palm, as the officer opened his door and positioned himself in the crack with his service weapon directed at Dash.

"Hands where I can see 'em," the officer demanded.

"My name is Dashiell West. I'm an agent with the Federal Bureau of Investigations, behavioral science unit. I'm holding my badge in my right palm." Dash kept his hands high in the air while awaiting permission to move.

The officer spoke into his radio and then waved Dash over. The two exchanged handshakes before

Dash gave a rundown of the situation. The officer relayed information over the radio, and Dash explained his theory about the rider having help nearby.

Another officer arrived on the scene, and while he was being filled in, Dash ran over to the SUV to check on Raina.

"Hey. Are you hanging in there all right?" he asked as she rolled down the passenger window.

"I've been better. Nothing a good glass of wine won't cure." Her calm demeanor caught him off guard. But then, she was remarkable in more ways than one.

"You've earned it," he said before reaching in and taking her hand in his. The connection sent more of those electrical currents racing through him. He ignored them.

"Any sign of him?" She stared down at his hand but didn't jerk away this time.

"No. He could be anywhere," he said.

"But he's hurt. He has to have a limp or damaged shoulder after taking that fall." Her observation was dead-on.

"That's my guess too."

"How did he get away so quickly? I mean, I definitely took a minute to regroup, but you were watching, aware," she said.

"Your guess is as good as mine there. He had to have had help."

"Which means he's not working alone," she stated.

"Afraid not." It didn't rule out Calum or his wife necessarily. They would have the resources to hire

someone. If Dash had to guess, this guy was professional, a hired gun. There was no way an amateur
could have taken that kind of fall and gotten back
up. He had to have been wearing some type of specialized body armor.

"Is he a hit man?" she asked point-blank.

The question caught him off guard. It probably
shouldn't have. She was astute, and it was a reason-
able assumption. "It's possible."

"Then we need to forget the wine and brew some
coffee. We can't stop until we figure out who is behind this." She pursed her lips. "Any chance we can
find a way to get your sister out on bail?"

"I highly doubt it," he said. "The very fact her
brother is a federal employee makes this whole
situation more complicated. Any whiff of special
treatment and my department will be under a mi-
croscope."

Raina pursed her lips. "She's in danger while she's
inside, isn't she?"

"Yes. But she would be in danger out here too,"
he pointed out.

"True. I can see that I am too." She paused for a
few beats. "I'll take you up on your offer to stay at
your place until we get to the bottom of this."

"I think that's wise." There was some relief in her
decision. But she was right about one thing: Layla
had never been in more danger. If she died in prison,
it could be made to look like a suicide. With Dash
out of the way, there would be no one to take up her
case. A cover-up could make this all go away. There

was a handful of people who could pull off this scale of attack: someone who was very well off, someone who was connected to organized crime or someone who was known for her ruthlessness. Greed or revenge. Those were two powerful motivators.

Miguel needed to be brought up to speed.

RAINA GAVE HER statement to the cops while Dash updated his boss. He reclaimed the driver's seat when it was all said and done.

"Are we still stopping by Stuart's?" she asked, figuring plans had changed.

Dash glanced at the clock. "I want a background check on Calum and his wife. Miguel is working on one for Stuart too. We're gathering everything we can find out about Talia. In the meantime, it's getting late. Let's swing by your place."

"Sounds like a plan."

The rest of the ride was spent in companionable silence. Raina was working through what had just happened and the frustration that came with seeing Layla locked behind bars and not being able to do anything about it. It was increasingly clear Layla had been set up.

There were the obvious people in their circle to consider. And then there was the outside chance the person who did this wasn't connected to Layla at all. Or the firm. She needed to expand her scope. Despite this feeling very personal, hackers could be anywhere. The breach could have been random.

The crazy part about it was Layla was too smart

to fall into the trap of clicking on a random link in her email or opening anything suspect. She had built custom firewalls and never kept virus-protection software on her system. She was too savvy to leave a back door on her computer the size of Texas. If she bought a new laptop, she immediately uninstalled all the bloatware and anything that could leave her system compromised.

A random hacker made less sense when she really thought about it but couldn't be excluded. Good hackers might be hard to come by, but they were sneaky. The ones who got through were brilliant minds.

An internal job made sense from a motive point of view, but again, Layla was no slacker in the brains department. Getting her password would be more than tricky. Was Calum that smart? No. He had the means to hire people who were. Unless he used his time at her apartment to snoop around.

But why? Two million dollars was a lot of money, don't get her wrong. But it wasn't much to a person in his position. Her immediate thought was that he wanted to discredit her. Mission accomplished there.

Dash drove to the pier and then lined up for the ferry. "Is your car waiting on the other side?"

"No, I rode my bike." And by *bike*, she meant the pedaling kind. She lived on Bainbridge Island in a garage apartment not far from the pier. The low-maintenance lifestyle was a no-brainer considering how much time she spent at the office. This way, she got to live somewhere she could have an incredible view without paying exorbitant prices. Plus, living there felt like she was on vacation on the weekends and away from the hustle and bustle of downtown Seattle. Yet Bainbridge Island was there, a short ferry ride away if she wanted to be around people.

Don't even get her started on the food on the island, which rivaled that of Seattle's. One of her favorite food haunts was in a gas station of all places. So a trip into town wasn't necessary for an amazing meal.

"We can leave my bike there. It'll be faster that way and it's chained, so no one will take it." There was very little theft on the island.

"Or better yet, I'll strap it on top and we can park it at your place."

"Sounds good to me." She was eager to get back to his place, get settled and roll up her sleeves. The motorcycle had been a wake-up call for them both—one she intended to answer by pulling out all the stops. She was a decent hacker when she put her mind to it. And she was more determined than ever to trace this jerk. Everyone left a trail in the tech world. It was just a matter of finding it, and they would get their guy.

Chapter Eleven

Dash parked next to the detached-garage apartment.
He hopped out of the SUV and brought the bike
down from the rack on top of his vehicle. The home-
owners gave Raina full use of the garage since there
was a stairwell from inside leading to her apartment. They always parked on the opposite side of
the house, giving Raina a decent amount of privacy
and the feeling of seclusion.

His cell buzzed in his pocket. He pulled it out
and checked the screen. "It's Miguel. Go ahead on
up and I'll be there after I find out what he wants."

Raina nodded and frowned. Her disappointment
was a gut punch. The truth was that he'd use any
excuse not to go inside her apartment. Although,
he was certain a night spent having sex with Raina
again would be a game changer, trumping every
other in his life. Once hadn't nearly been enough and
he'd had to draw on all his self-control to walk away.

"Hey, Miguel. What's up?" Dash had a low-key
relationship with his boss outside of the office, where
they could be less formal.

"After you briefed me on your chat with Layla's boss, I called him. I was a hundred percent certain he was hiding something, so I asked for a meeting," Miguel said.

"How'd that go over?"

"The guy was shaking in his shoes when I dropped by his office. After a little more digging and a lot more persuading, he admitted the investment bank may have been hacked a few days before the embezzlement," Miguel stated.

"He was definitely covering for something or someone while I was there. I had all the vibes that he was about to crack before he made certain I was escorted out of the building." Was this what Alec had been hiding? Was he involved?

"After his slip—there was no way he intended to give me that much information, by the way—so, after, he has me escorted out and then gives me the number of his attorney."

"Innocent people rarely lawyer up so fast," Dash pointed out.

"Your visit must have left him thinking about his own personal responsibility in this should it all go south."

"Did you visit him in his office?" Dash asked.

"Yes, but then he asked to go for a walk."

Interesting. Dash noted the change of venue. "He's connected."

"As in, organized crime?"

"Has pictures of crime bosses in his office along with celebrities and politicians," Dash said.

"His background needs to be thoroughly vetted." Miguel didn't mess around.

"I couldn't agree more." Dash wanted everything, from where he went to grade school to his major in college. Miguel would deliver.

"The vice president of human resources, Linda Ramirez, is fully cooperating. She is having her team pull together a list of employees and their jobs. She's willing to turn over the résumés of everyone at the firm."

"I'm assuming you asked for anyone with a technical background first." Dash knew Miguel would dot every *i* and cross every *t*.

"That's right. We'll start there. Not just with people who have technical jobs but everyone in the company with a tech degree," Miguel said.

"Just so you know, Raina Andress is under my protection," Dash said.

"She was on my list of people to circle back to," Miguel admitted.

"Ask me anything you want to know. Or, I can bring her into the office," Dash offered.

"Write up a report instead," Miguel said. "Have it in my inbox before I go into the office tomorrow morning."

"Will do, sir."

The two finished their conversation and then ended the call. Dash stood in the gravel, looking up at what would be Raina's bedroom window. He grabbed the bike and, on a heavy sigh, headed toward the garage.

He found a spot for the bike before shuffling up the stairs. The door to her apartment was left open, so he walked inside.

The place was Raina to a T. Most of the colors were neutral, the furniture was the kind he could sink into, and there was a pop of a vibrant shade of blue in every room. It was cozy, and there was a small patio off the master bedroom with views of the Sound. The island itself was lush with greenery everywhere he turned.

He'd thought about buying a place out here before settling downtown where the action was. Being here now, he wondered if he'd made a mistake. Or was it just this place that had him feeling like he was missing out on something?

The cozy one-bedroom apartment was the perfect weekend getaway.

"I'm in here." Raina didn't have to shout to be heard. He was trying to avoid a trip into her bedroom.

Thinking of her in bed didn't help on the follow-through of pushing her away. His plan had worked, and he'd never been more disappointed. It was for the best the two of them didn't try to follow through on the attraction simmering between them. For one, it would have jeopardized her relationship with Layla. His would survive but would Raina's? Layla needed her best friend, and he was determined not to mess that up for her. He'd done enough damage not being there for his sister when he should have been, and the guilt was crushing.

When Dash had brought Layla to his place, he'd put her on a rigid routine. It might have gotten her on the right track in a whole lot of ways, but he'd never given her the chance to talk about how she felt after losing their parents. He was starting to learn how important talking was. Losing their parents had been hard on Dash as an adult. Layla was still a child, for all intents and purposes.

"I'm almost ready." There was an uncertainty to Raina's voice that led him to believe she was unsure why he was still in the living room instead of with her in the bedroom. Part of him wanted to walk right in there and plant the biggest kiss on her lips just to prove to them both the white-hot attraction that had been simmering between them could be managed. It might be a slow-burning fire but that didn't mean it had to get out of hand. They were adults with plenty of self-control to draw from. Besides, willpower wasn't normally something Dash grappled with. Not even when he was barely old enough to have hair on his chest did he lack resolve to command his impulses.

If he didn't prove that fact to himself right now, he would regret it. Besides, he and Raina were about to spend twenty-four seven together, in close quarters, for the foreseeable future. Walking into the next room and planting a kiss on those thick cherry lips of hers would be doing them both a favor. Clearing the elephant in the room, so to speak.

So that's exactly what he did. He walked right

into the bedroom, straight up to her, and took her wrists in his hands.

He locked gazes with her, searching for permission to move forward or a rebuke that would make him take a step back to reevaluate.

Those sky-blue eyes of hers glittered with something that looked a lot like need. He took it as a sign to move forward. That, and the fact that her tongue darted across her bottom lip like she was about to welcome him home. The silky trail her tongue left behind mesmerized him for a few seconds.

And then he tugged her toward him, locked on to her gaze and brought those gorgeous lips of hers to meet his. The split-second moan of pleasure she gave was enough to tell him he was moving in the right direction.

He loved the feeling of her lips moving against his. He let go of her wrists to bring his hands up to the soft skin of her cheeks. He framed her face with his hands and tilted her head to the right for better access.

His pulse pounded and his breath quickened.

She parted her lips for him as she brought her hands up to his shoulders, digging her nails into him as though to ground herself.

A groan escaped before he could reel it in when he let his tongue dart inside her mouth. She had a mix of coffee and peppermint on her tongue. Those weren't two flavors he would normally put together, but they worked wonders on her, driving him to a whole new level of desire.

An ache formed in his chest. He'd never gone from zero to a hundred-and-ten-miles-an-hour before, usually preferring a long, slow buildup. With Raina, everything was different. He'd thought about that sexy pout of her lips more than he wanted to acknowledge since the last time they'd been together.

It was probably just two broken people finding a way to fit together that drew him to her on a soul-deep level. Dash didn't normally do soul-deep with anyone. He preferred 'at a distance' when it came to emotional connections.

She teased his tongue inside her mouth, and the temptation to pick her up and take two steps to the bed was a physical force.

He denied it. This time. The kisses they'd shared before ranked at the top of his list, but these were somehow better. He wasn't sure if it had anything to do with the old saying about absence making the heart grow fonder, but he wondered if the same axiom worked for sexual desire too. Because right now, he was committed, with the full knowledge this decision would come back to bite him.

THE IMAGE OF Layla in the awful jumpsuit was the equivalent of a bucket of ice being thrown over Raina's head. She pulled back from Dash, hating that their lips were no longer touching. As far as kisses went, she'd never experienced anything that came close to a Dash kiss.

What was that saying about forbidden fruit? It must apply here, and she finally understood the depths to which it could go. Because she'd gotten lost in in a matter of seconds.

There was so much heat and passion in the kiss they were both left trying to catch their breath. He leaned in and rested his forehead on hers.

"Damn," was all he managed to say in between heated breaths and was exactly the same word she was thinking.

Damn is about right. The next word that came to mind was *damned*, which brought her to *cursed*. Their relationship was cursed. It had stopped even before it got started despite the best night of her life followed by the worst morning after.

They couldn't afford to take their focus off the investigation while Layla sat in prison. In fact, it was probably the near-death experience that had them grasping at life with both hands. She'd read about that phenomenon. There was an article about baby booms after towns were hit with a catastrophic event. People needed proof that life would go on at the most primal level.

So she'd blame biology for the temporary lapse in judgment.

"That can't happen again, Dash." She didn't say that her heart couldn't take it, but it was true.

"I know." There was a lot of sadness and resignation in his voice.

"As long as we're both clear on that point," she said.

He nodded against her forehead.

"Then, after this, we have to stop." She tilted her

head and captured his bottom lip in between her teeth. She sucked and then tugged.

His reaction was instantaneous. He looped his arms around her waist, pressing her body flush with his, and lifted her off her feet.

His tongue drove inside her mouth, causing her pulse to shoot through the roof and desire to temporarily weaken her knees.

He kissed her so thoroughly that when he set her back down, she couldn't hold her own weight. She finally understood what people referred to when they mentioned a bone-melting kiss. She'd mistakenly believed no one could make her bones feel like butter before Dash. And kissing him a second time around was proving even more potent.

She wanted nothing more than to live in this moment, to freeze time and stay here for just a little while longer. Rationalizations floated across her mind that tried to justify giving in to the power and masculinity that was Dashiell West. But she recognized them for what they were. Excuses.

Raina wanted nothing more than to strip down bare in front of Dash and spend the next couple of days exploring each other.

They didn't have time. And it was a bad idea for so many reasons beyond that.

He pulled back. He searched her eyes, and it was as though an entire conversation happened between them in those few seconds without a word needing to be spoken. They both wanted this to happen more than they wanted air.

But Layla. She needed and deserved their undivided attention. Beyond that, she wouldn't approve of a fling between her best friend and her brother.

Raina tucked a loose tendril of hair behind her ear and regrouped. She took in a slow breath and tried to clear the fog that consumed her when she was this close to Dash. The man was smart, capable and smokin' hot. Those were just a few of his obvious qualities. She could only imagine what sex would be like this time around, based on the heat in the few kisses they'd shared.

And that's exactly where sex between them needed to stay: in her imagination.

Packing. She'd been packing when he'd charged into the room and kissed her. "I'm almost done with my overnight bag." Her voice was a little deeper and more gravelly.

"I'll just wait in the living room."

A sound in the next room caused her to freeze and Dash to reach for his holstered weapon. He brought out his firearm, pivoted and had her against the wall with his left hand holding her behind him. It had happened in a matter of seconds, and she'd barely gotten her wits back.

Granted, his training had clearly kicked in, but she didn't like the feeling of needing to rely on someone else's quick thinking for protection. The flyer for the personal-protection class would be fished out of her trash can when this was all over. She was going to call and set up her first lesson. This feeling of helplessness was for the birds, and she was clearly out of her league with motorcycle dude. She had no plans to be caught off guard again. She'd frozen when she should have defended. Having her safety challenged for the first time sent her mind spinning.

Dash brought his left hand up to his mouth and his index finger to his lips. He was telling her to be quiet. Then he indicated she should stay put. Little did he know she had no intention of moving until he said it was safe to do so. She wasn't stupid and didn't have a death wish.

He inched toward the door with the stealth and grace of an alley cat moving along the shadows. Soundlessly, he disappeared down the hall. The noise had probably just been the wind or the floors settling. It happened all the time, she reminded herself.

It wasn't until he appeared in the doorway again that she exhaled.

"All clear," he said. "But I should have locked the door when I came inside."

"The wind?" she asked, thinking how dangerous his job truly was. Her own father had been a US marine. She'd grown up a military brat until middle school, when he was killed during active duty. A shudder rocketed through her at the memory. She never talked about her father. As far as she was concerned, he was a closed subject.

"Let's go," Raina said, ready to get out of there.

Dash nodded and reached for her hand. She pulled away before he made contact and grabbed her suitcase.

"Do you mind?" She handed over her small suit-

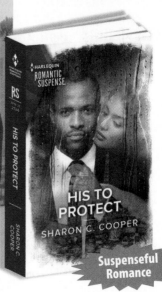

Get up to 4
FREE FABULOUS BOOKS
You Love!

To thank you for being a loyal reader we'd like to send you up to 4 FREE BOOKS, absolutely free.

Just write "YES" on the Loyal Reader Voucher and we'll send you up to 4 Free Books and Free Mystery Gifts, altogether worth over $20, as a way of saying thank you for being a loyal reader.

Try **Harlequin® Romantic Suspense** books featuring heart-racing page-turners with unexpected plot twists and irresistible chemistry that will keep you guessing to the very end.

Try **Harlequin Intrigue® Larger-Print** books featuring action-packed stories that will keep you on the edge of your seat. Solve the crime and deliver justice at all costs.

Or **TRY BOTH!**

We are so glad you love the books as much as we do and can't wait to send you great new books.

So don't miss out, return your Loyal Reader Voucher Today!

Pam Powers

LOYAL READER
FREE BOOKS VOUCHER

YES! I Love Reading, please send me up to 4 FREE BOOKS and Free Mystery Gifts from the series I select.

Just write in "YES" on the dotted line below then return this card today and we'll send your free books & gifts asap!

➡ YES ⬅

Which do you prefer?

☐ **Harlequin®
Romantic
Suspense**
240/340 HDL GRHP

☐ **Harlequin
Intrigue®
Larger-Print**
199/399 HDL GRHP

☐ **BOTH**
240/340 & 199/399
HDL GRHZ

FIRST NAME

LAST NAME

ADDRESS

APT.#

CITY

STATE/PROV.

ZIP/POSTAL CODE

EMAIL ☐ Please check this box if you would like to receive newsletters and promotional emails from Harlequin Enterprises ULC and its affiliates. You can unsubscribe anytime.

HI/HRS-520-LR21

case to him, knowing he would want to carry it anyway.

"Okay," was all he said, but the disappointment in his eyes at her jerking her hand away was what nearly killed her. But so did ending that all-consuming kiss and desire for another.

Chapter Twelve

Dash stretched his arms, sore from sitting in the same position too long. He glanced at the clock. Both he and Raina had been at it for three solid hours with no breaks. It was almost four o'clock in the morning. His coffee had gone cold hours ago, and he needed to make a pit stop in the bathroom.

He suppressed a yawn and then stood. "Can I get you anything while I'm up?"

"More coffee would be amazing." She didn't look up. She'd been acting different ever since the kiss at her place. He'd been swept up with memories and had let himself get out of hand. Control and self-discipline weren't normally an issue for him, so he'd been thrown off by how fast he'd snapped into primal mode.

"With a little cream?" he asked.

"Yes." An eyebrow hiked up, and she looked surprised that he remembered how she took her coffee. But that was all she said. She sat on the opposite end of the couch, as far from him as humanly possible while still sitting on the actual sofa.

He couldn't say he didn't deserve the cold shoulder he'd been getting ever since her apartment. He was normally the guy who ditched when emotions got complicated. Trying to convince himself he felt this way because she was his sister's best friend fell flat.

In the bathroom, he slapped his face with cold water and only then realized he still had on slacks and a button-down shirt. Jeans and a cotton T-shirt were more his style, so he moved into the master bedroom and changed into something more comfortable. He fired off a couple of push-ups to get the blood pumping again. Sitting for too long was taking a toll. He needed to run down to the gym and get in a workout. He could think better there, but he wasn't quite ready to leave Raina by herself. She'd had her head down, working hard, and he wanted to keep the momentum going for both of them.

He brewed a couple cups of coffee. He took his black, mainly because he didn't like to waste time with fixings and he liked the bitter taste on his tongue. He brought one over to Raina and set it down in front of her.

She bristled when he got close. He didn't like it.

"I owe you an apology for what happened last night. I was out of line at your apartment," he started.

"It's fine, Dash." In his experience, when someone said *it's fine*, the opposite was usually true.

"We don't have to talk about it if you don't want to." He exhaled, searching for the right words. He was in new territory, but her understanding that attraction had nothing to do with the reason why he'd pushed her away before was important.

"I'd rather not, if that's okay with you."

Before he could respond, his cell indicated an email had come through. He'd put a notification on his team-member contacts, so this might be important.

He took a couple of steps to the opposite end of the sofa and settled down with his coffee. He took a sip, enjoying the burn, and then pulled up his email on the TV screen turned monitor.

The encrypted message was from Liam.

Turns out the firm was hacked two days before Layla supposedly embezzled the money. Social security numbers, investment account numbers, names.

Raina scooted over and then studied the screen. "My department wasn't notified of this security breech."

"Why wouldn't they tell you?" he asked.

"My boss can be secretive. We might all be under investigation internally if something like this happened," she said.

"Layla's boss didn't fully cooperate because he must not want the news of the hacking to get out. Very sensitive and valuable data was captured by the hacker, according to Liam." This kind of leak could bankrupt a financial-services company if high-profile accounts were closed.

"I'm wondering if this person framed Layla, or

did they simply 'open' a door to steal her password that someone else took advantage of?" She finally glanced over at him. "We both know that some hackers are in it for the prize of hacking in and of itself, not to steal or destroy. Some are in it for both."

"The trick is to figure out what we're dealing with here. Someone who opened a door and then walked away for someone else to walk right in?" He was thinking out loud, but it was nice to work with someone who understood tech. And if he was being honest, it was nice to be around Raina. Better than nice. He'd missed her. And Dash never missed people.

"This all gives me the feeling that whoever we're dealing with either works at the firm or has an in. No one should be able to get into our system at all. It's supposed to be foolproof. It has the highest level of encryption and security protocols in place," she said.

As expected when dealing with high profile people and more money than Dash would see in his lifetime—which was saying something considering the number of zeroes in his investment account. He'd offered to let Layla manage his money, and she'd refused so fast his head was still spinning. She told him she wanted to make herself successful on her own terms, and she'd never be able to do that if she continued to ride his coattails. At first blush, he thought she was worried about losing his money and the awkwardness that would follow their relationship. It would be no fun sitting across the Thanksgiving table from her brother if she'd just lost his life savings. Dash had full trust in her and didn't view it that way, but she would. She was as stubborn as she was determined, a sometimes difficult combination but one that resulted in quite a few millionaires over the years. It took both to be truly successful. One had to be tenacious enough to shut out the world and a little bit selfish too. Determination meant there was no plan B. There was only a plan A, and there was no room for failure. Obstinacy applied to creating the kind of discipline it took to go after a goal could be a very good thing. Applied poorly, and it could just fast-track someone to bankruptcy.

Layla had always said she would either end up eating peanut butter sandwiches every day or lobster. There wasn't a whole lot of middle ground for her. That trait was how he knew she would achieve great things. Things that would either make her rich or land her in jail. That had been the joke between the two of them, which wasn't so funny anymore.

"Call me crazy, but I have this feeling we're looking for someone who works at the firm," Raina said.

"It's possible someone paid an employee or intern for access. Grab anyone's credentials and the hacker could have a little look-see. Snoop around the system and poke until they found holes," he pointed out.

She was nodding. And talking to him again, which he liked more than he wanted to admit. The two of them made a good team.

"There's an attachment," Raina said, pointing to the screen.

"Yes." He scrolled down to bring it into view. It was a spreadsheet marked Employee Info.

That was more like it. Dash clicked on the file and the data filled the screen. Two hundred and seventeen employees. Most hedge funds were small businesses, not more than a couple dozen people total. The larger ones employed a thousand. This was on the lower end of the midsize spectrum.

The file housed names and background information like degrees and interests.

"We're looking for anyone with an IT background—"

"You do realize that makes me a suspect," Raina quipped.

"I'm aware. You're also offering your support for the investigation and so that puts you at the bottom of the list," he said.

"It would be too ironic for someone to use my credentials to set up my best friend. Anyone internally would have to know that would never happen," she said.

Raina being his sister's best friend was by far the biggest complication to having a relationship with her. Or was that just a cop-out? He quieted the little voice in his head that was trying to say he couldn't handle a relationship with a person like Raina. She shattered all the preconceived notions about the people he spent time with, about himself. Normally, he wasn't a talker, but here he was staying up all night talking to her.

There was no alcohol to blame. No lapse in judgment. He had full-on and willingly wanted to spend the night *talking* to her. Talking. He let the thought sit for a long moment before shoving it to the background. The kisses they'd shared weren't so easily dismissed. They wanted him to think about how incredible the coffee would taste on her lips now as she took a sip.

"So, let's start with your department," he said. "How many employees are there in IT?"

"We have a dozen current employees, and we had an intern whose time was up recently. We tried to convince him to stay, but he had other offers. Ones we couldn't compete with, no matter how much my boss tried," she said.

"What did you think of the guy?"

"His technical abilities were on point. No doubt he had the goods. I didn't think he was the greatest personality fit. We all get along. You know how it is in most IT departments. I don't have to tell you the comradery that exists," she said.

"I remember those days. The 'us against them' mentality," he said with a hint of nostalgia creeping in.

"Yeah, well, he was a snitch. He apparently kept a spreadsheet of when each one of us went to lunch and then came back. A couple of the guys like to take a long lunch to work out, and he documented that too," she said. "The problem was that he left it up on his screen once when he went to the bathroom. You know how tech people can be—razzing each other mercilessly."

Dash nodded and cracked a smile. Lots of pranks.

"Leaving your phone lying around without a lock screen was basically suicide."

"Everyone started being tough on this kid, even though he swore it was for a school project and that he had no intentions of turning it in to the boss," she said. And then her brow furrowed like when the wheels were turning in the back of her mind.

"You don't think…" She paused for a couple of beats. "It wouldn't be him…right?"

"WHAT'S THE KID'S NAME?"

"Sheldon Kylo," Raina supplied.

Raina didn't want to believe Sheldon was capable of doing something like this. Employees were well vetted. Was the company more lax when it came to interns, assuming these young people had reached at least the barrier of being in an A-list tech program? They only recruited from the best schools.

"Do you have access to samples of any of his code?" Dash asked, his fingers already busy on the keyboard.

"As a matter of fact, he worked on a project for me." She pulled up the company system and located the project file.

Dash scooted closer, and his warm spicy scent washed over her, bringing parts of her to life she needed to find a way to ignore. Reminding her brain Dash was off-limits wasn't helping as much as she wanted it to. Her stomach free-fell, and electric currents raced through her where his shoulder touched hers.

"Here you go." She tilted the screen toward him.

He studied it with the intensity of a star quarterback memorizing a game-winning play. "Okay. I got it."

Everyone had a unique signature when it came to coding, a particular stamp known only to them. It was a lot like handwriting. No one made identical loops on *L*s or held the pen in the exact same way. Coding was no different. There was a lot of personal preference and skill that went into it.

Dash pulled up the lines of code that were responsible for his sister's imprisonment. He checked her monitor, but after a few seconds of scrolling, neither one needed to continue. They did, though, needing to be certain.

"Sheldon?" She heard the disbelief in her own voice. And then a picture snapped together of a young guy who was probably smarter than all of them. He might have targeted Layla by installing something on her computer to record her keystrokes. "He would have had access to the systems."

She didn't need to explain the rest to Dash, because he probably got there faster than she did.

He raked his fingers through his hair and then rubbed the scruff on his chin. He bit out a few choice words—the same ones Raina was thinking.

"When did he leave the firm?" he asked.

"A few weeks ago," she said. "Maybe a month."

"Did he leave on good terms?"

"Yes, overall. The boss liked him and tried to get him to stay. He went through the motions, pretending to be flattered at the offer, and I believe he even said he needed to think about it."

"But he didn't take it," Dash pointed out.

She shook her head. "No. In the end he said he really liked working there, but the other offer was a lot more lucrative."

"Do you know where he ended up taking a job?" he asked.

"It was a start-up by the name of the Money Fund. They were offering stock options, and he said he wanted to be part of building something from scratch."

"Two million dollars would certainly soften the blow if the fund didn't make it off the ground," he said.

"He could do his own thing with that kind of money. He could use it as seed money for his own company." She pulled up the website for the Money Fund.

She scrolled through the company's site until she located the employees. There he was: Sheldon Kylo. His title was VP of Development.

"Not a bad gig for a snot-nosed kid barely out of college," Dash said.

"He skipped a year in school and then graduated college in three years instead of the usual four. He's working on an advanced degree." She remembered how bright he was and how much he kept to himself.

"I think it's time we pay him a visit at his home."

Chapter Thirteen

Sheldon Kylo's apartment was a two-room addition to the back of a house on Twenty-Fourth Avenue South where the road met up with South Spokane Street. It sat on a corner lot adjacent to Jefferson Park and was located southeast of the city near the industrial district.

Dash brought his sports car in case the need arose to zip through traffic quickly, but there was no drama on the ride over.

The sun was rising, and there was a light on inside the small apartment. A subcompact electric car was parked in front of the door. Dash figured these were good signs Sheldon was home.

He knocked on the door three times. Three taps in rapid succession.

"Mr. Kylo, my name is Special Agent Dash West," he said, using his authoritative voice. "We know you are home, so you might as well open up."

The door swung open, and a very agitated young man stood there with a scornful look on his face. His skin was sallow. He was tall and looked like he hadn't quite filled out yet. His arms looked more like rubber bands than anything else. He wore a wrinkled T-shirt depicting a grimacing middle finger. His gaze shifted from Dash to Raina, and then his shoulders sagged.

"What are you doing here?" Now he sounded put out. "I walked away from that job."

"I'd like to ask you a few questions," Dash said.

"You can start by answering mine." Sheldon glared at Raina. "What is she doing here?"

The kid didn't seem scared or guilty. Then again, with an IQ that had him finishing both high school and college a year early, he might be the smartest guy in the room. Duly noted. What the kid had in IQ, Dash had in experience.

Sheldon leaned into the doorjamb and held the door close to his body, effectively blocking their view to the inside of his place.

"You know Raina Andress," Dash countered. He pulled his badge from his hip clip and showed it to Sheldon.

People reacted one of two ways when they saw that badge: they were either scared or relieved. Sheldon was indifferent. Like Dash had just shown him a test grade that came out to a C in a class like PE.

Sheldon almost looked like he'd been expecting the visit, but Dash must be misreading him. A cocky kid like this would never accept that someone with a lesser IQ than him would catch on to him.

"Did you interact with Layla West during your

internship at Baker Financial?" Dash continued, not missing a beat.

"No. Why?" His bland gray eyes suddenly sparked. "Oh. Right. The person who embezzled two million dollars?"

"How do you know about the case?" Dash asked.

"It's all over the news," he said with a nonchalant shrug.

Dash took note that Sheldon knew the exact amount of money missing. Of course, two million dollars would seem like a lot of money to most people.

"Can we come in, Mr. Kylo?" Dash didn't figure the answer would be yes, but it was always worth asking.

"For what?" Sheldon's face wrinkled like he'd just eaten a pickled prune.

"To ask you a few questions." Dash studied Sheldon. The kid was cocky. Whoever pulled this stunt was cocky. So he had that in common. Was he smart enough to pull off this kind of job?

"Can't you ask them with me standing right here?" Sheldon didn't seem like he was going to budge.

"We'd be more comfortable inside," Dash pressed.

"I wouldn't." Sheldon sounded like a spoiled kid used to getting his way. Geniuses could be like that, and Sheldon seemed to fit the bill. Was he devious too?

A kid like this would pull this kind of stunt just to see if he could get away with it. In college, there was a group of brilliant high school students who had a special dorm and lived on campus rather than at home for their last two years of high school. In turn, they received college credit and most ended up in the Ivys after graduation. They were full-ride kids who got into the best-of-the-best schools without blinking an eye. There was a scandal that brought federal investigators on campus involving those bright kids. If Dash was honest, it was the first time he'd thought about joining the federal ranks. But the brainiacs figured out that vending machines discerned dollar bills by measuring the distance between the president's eyes. So they made copies of dollar bills and had a weekend full of junk food and endless sodas. Well, endless until the machines emptied.

Two days later, the feds showed up. The kids, still minors, were issued stern warnings and told a file was now open on them that would follow them for the next ten years. He'd heard that one of the kids peed himself during an interview. The agents handled the kids with a mix of authority and kindness, and not one crossed the street without using a crosswalk afterward.

The minute Dash looked up salaries, he'd decided to stick to computer science as a major. But those agents had always stayed with him, and now he was proud to have joined their ranks.

"I don't have to let you in. I know my rights," Sheldon said with a pout.

"Why would you go looking up your rights, Mr. Kylo?" Dash figured this was a good time to push a little bit.

"I, um, I just figured it's always a good thing to know." The question had shaken Sheldon.

"Really? That's interesting because I rarely come across innocent people who can spout their rights. In fact, most of the time, they're cooperative." Dash issued one of his legendary smiles meant to disarm. "The last interview I was on, the woman I spoke to had fresh brownies from the oven. She practically forced me to sit at her table and eat one. She had the best fresh-brewed coffee in the state."

"Well, I'm not her."

"Clearly. She was eager to be a helpful witness," Dash said. The last word caused Sheldon to perk up a bit.

"What do you want to know? Ask away." He folded his arms across his chest. His legs were crossed at the ankles. His body language was clear. He shut down faster than a restaurant after a listeria outbreak.

"Why did you leave?" Dash asked.

"Easy. I got a better offer." Based on the certainty in his voice and the rapid nature of his response, Dash counted that answer as true.

Dash continued down that line of questioning. "What made the offer better?"

"Money. Atmosphere. Those are just the top two reasons." Sheldon looked proud of himself.

"Tell me about the atmosphere at Baker. Did you like your coworkers?" Dash knew the answer to this question.

"Not really." Sheldon got bonus points for his honesty in Dash's book.

"Why not?"

"They weren't very accepting of me. I didn't get the impression they liked me," he quipped.

"What about Layla West? Did she like you?"

"She didn't have a reason not to," he answered quickly. He must have thought these answers through in advance—not exactly the action of an innocent person. Or maybe he'd been expecting someone to show up at his door eventually once the news broke.

"How well did you know her?" Dash asked.

"Not very well. She wasn't in my department."

"How long did you intern?" Dash continued.

"The summer," he supplied.

"Isn't the whole reason for an internship to get a job offer at the end of the term?" Unless things had changed, that was the way they did it in Dash's day. Of course, he'd been out of school almost a decade, and it seemed like times had changed overnight.

"Kind of." Sheldon pursed his lips and narrowed his gaze. "That's a narrow viewpoint, though."

"Educate me."

"Internships are a way for a candidate to get to know a company and vice versa. I was checking to see if the company was a good fit for me as much as they were seeing if I had the right skill set. Obviously, I didn't want to work with a group of people who thought it was funny to pour plant water in my bottle of Coke the minute I left my cubicle unattended." Sheldon glared at Raina now. "I had a motion-activated camera set up on my laptop."

"I can't speak for the others, but I had nothing to do with that," she said. "And if you truly had a camera set up, I don't have to tell you that I wasn't involved."

Sheldon didn't seem to care. He lumped everyone into the same category... Jerk. He was also making a case for motive: revenge.

"Sounds like the team underestimated you," Dash said.

"Darn right they did. But I got them back." Sheldon seemed exceptionally proud of himself. He was immature and that had Dash wondering if he would slash someone's tires, not steal two million bucks to prove a point.

"How did you do that, Mr. Kylo?" Dash leaned in. "By getting revenge on the whole company?"

"No. Why would I do that?" Sheldon's face twisted up. "I gave the footage to HR on my way out and told them to ask the department why I refused to work there."

The kid was angry. He was brilliant. The question was, how far would he go?

"Are you aware there was a breach of security recently at the firm?" Dash figured he'd throw it out there and see how the kid reacted. "It would take someone with inside knowledge of how the system worked to pull off a stunt like that."

Recognition dawned and Sheldon immediately

started backpedaling. "Hey, I had nothing to do with stealing money."

"Why don't you try and convince me? Because right now, I'm about to read you your rights and take you for a drive." Dash wouldn't, but part of being a good investigator was knowing when to push and when to retreat. This was the time to push. The kid had been knocked off the pedestal he'd put himself on.

"I should get an attorney," Sheldon threatened in a voice that sounded like the equivalent of tattling on the playground.

Dash crossed his arms over his chest. "You certainly have that right."

Sheldon stood there for a moment, looking like he was debating his next actions carefully.

Dash decided it was time to push. "In my experience, innocent people don't usually resort to calling an attorney over answering a few questions to clear up a misunderstanding or help with an investigation."

"Well, I just want to make sure what you're doing is legal," Sheldon defended.

"Oh, rest assured, I would never break the law."

"BUT YOU WOULD violate company policy without blinking an eye, which proves you're not opposed to bending the rules." Raina had heard enough from Sheldon. She wasn't convinced of his innocence, and he was acting like a spoiled jerk.

"What is that supposed to mean?"

"Spying on your coworkers, Sheldon? Are you

trying to tell me that's ethical? I can promise you it's a violation of the employee handbook, and I happen to know you were provided a copy of the rules," she shot back.

Dash rocked back on his heels. "A jury wouldn't take lightly to information like that."

"Hold on a minute…" There was a wild quality to his eyes. If this jerk was the reason her best friend was behind bars, Raina was going to lose it right then and there. He couldn't hide behind that laissez-faire attitude for long when she knew a scared kid was behind the holier-than-thou arrogance.

"Why? You're acting guilty. You seem like you're guilty. Case closed." She was goading him for a reaction. "Do you really think they won't figure out you hacked into the system? We did. It's why we're here in the first place. Do you know how fast a guy like you will be eaten up in prison? Seriously, Sheldon. You think what my colleagues did to you was bad? Just wait."

"But I didn't do anything," he whined. She was clearly getting to him now. His demeanor shifted from cocky to deflated.

"Prove it," was all she said.

"I saw your code, man. I know it was you who hacked into the system a few days before the money disappeared." Dash chose that moment to pull zip cuffs from his back pocket. It was brilliant teamwork. He started spouting Miranda rights to Sheldon.

"Come inside." Sheldon walked away, leaving the door open.

Chapter Fourteen

"After you."

Raina took a couple of steps ahead of Dash and inside Sheldon's apartment. The place wasn't much bigger than the picture window to the right of the door. A black sofa was pushed up against the wall, and a small fridge/freezer combo was beside it. There were three racks above it. On the bottom one sat a microwave.

With Dash's wingspan, he could probably face the couch, extend his hands as far as they could go and touch opposite walls with his fingertips.

There was a makeshift table with two folding chairs on the other side of the room, along with a stove and more of those racks set up for clothing. The laptop sitting on top of the table probably cost more than all the furniture combined, probably the appliances too. There were three stacks of pennies on the table next to his laptop.

A floor lamp in one corner was the main light source.

Sheldon motioned toward the table. Raina moved

over to it and sat in one of the folding chairs. Dash leaned against the wall next to the door, so Sheldon took the vacant seat. He slumped forward and put his face in his hands.

He issued a sharp breath, and when he looked up at Raina, guilt was written all over his face. "Okay. Here's what happened." Sheldon looked like he was fighting back tears. "I've been following the story because I did something I probably shouldn't have, and I was scared something like this would happen." The anguish on his face was palpable. "I didn't mean to do anything bad, and I never expected to be able to hack into the system. I swear that I didn't do anything with the social security numbers or the accounts."

"Why should I believe you?" Dash was scrutinizing Sheldon, and the kid looked like he was about to break down. This was a far cry from the overconfident jerk who'd opened the door. Raina wondered if the kid could turn his emotions on and off on a dime.

"Because I'm telling the truth." His mouth twisted and his chin quivered. He was definitely holding back tears at this point.

"Go on," Dash urged, his voice a study in calm.

"Like I said, I never expected to be able to get into the system," he said.

"Then why do it at all?" Dash would already know the answer to that question. Raina did, as well. It was for the thrill.

"Because I could. To show them I could still keep

tabs on them if I wanted to." His gaze bounced from Dash to Raina and back.

"What else did you do while you were there? Leave a back door open?" Dash asked.

"No. They closed it. I can't get back in," he admitted.

Dash stood there for a long moment before finally pushing off the wall using his shoulder. "Don't leave town. I'll be keeping a close eye on you, and my boss will most likely want to bring you in for questioning at a later time."

"Breaking into the system just because you can will land you behind bars, Sheldon. I may not have gotten to know you while you were interning, but that doesn't mean I want you to make a stupid mistake," Raina said.

"Does that mean I'm in the clear?" he asked.

"Not exactly," Dash said. "For now, you're classified as a witness. The firm will most likely come after you for damages once we report our findings. They might scream for an indictment. You'll just have to wait and see on that one." Dash stopped at the door and then turned back. "It's a good idea for you to get a lawyer at this point."

That comment started the waterworks that had been brimming. "I swear I didn't mean to hurt anyone."

"Maybe a judge will go easy on you. You're young," Dash said. "Or the judge might decide to make an example out of you. Keep your nose clean in the meantime. It'll help your case in the long run."

Outside, Raina immediately noticed the tires on Dash's expensive sports car had been slashed.

Dash muttered a few choice words as he walked the perimeter of his vehicle. "They got all four in—" he checked his watch "—less than fifteen minutes."

Whoever did this had followed them. Raina had almost thought they made it to their destination a little too easily after the motorcycle incident. Was this Talia's handiwork?

Dash made a quick phone call to a tow truck and then to Liam, asking for a ride. "Did you leave anything inside the car?"

"No. My purse is right here, and my cell has been in my hand the whole time." She held it up as if he needed proof.

"What's that on the passenger seat, then?" One of his dark eyebrows arched as he made his way over to the side where she'd been sitting.

More of those curse words flew as he immediately surveyed the area, moving to put his body in between hers and the street.

"What is it?" Raina asked. He must've seen something to rattle him to this degree.

"A black rose," he said. "It's from her."

So, it was Talia. A cold chill raced down Raina's spine, gripping her with icy fingers. "Are you sure?"

"She used to threaten that if I got into a serious relationship with someone, she would know and she would make me suffer. A black rose is the way I would know it was her," he said.

"Could she have been responsible for the motorcycle incident?" *Incident* was a light way of putting what had happened, but it was the only word that came to mind.

"It's possible but I doubt it."

"How can you be so certain?" she asked.

He gave her a look of apology before saying, "Because the shooter was going after me. She would never do that. She said that I would be around to watch and suffer."

Part of her—and maybe it was that wishful-thinking piece—wondered if that played into his decision to walk out after their amazing night together. It was probably just her ego talking, but she wondered if he believed he'd be placing her in the line of fire if he let their relationship continue.

Taking down Layla would be the ultimate punishment for Dash. Anyone who knew him for more than five minutes knew how much he loved his sister. Talia would know that too. She'd been out of prison for six months. She'd been circling Dash, no doubt keeping tabs on his every move. Biding her time.

Talia was smart, according to Dash. She had coding skills. She could have used the back door Sheldon had created when he hacked into the system. She could have taken advantage of the hole he had created.

But one question remained, and it was a very big question: Where was the two million dollars?

Here were the facts: they'd had a break-in at work. The person had used Layla's password to move money. The trail had gone cold as soon as the money left the accounts. How had two million dollars just vanished into thin air?

Sheldon was guilty of hacking into the system, but he was shaking in his boots once serious questioning started and he realized how much trouble he could get in. Hacking into the system was going to have a consequence if the company decided to press charges. This information would have to go in Dash's report.

Before she could continue down the path much longer, a tow truck pulled up. As the sports car was being hitched onto the back, an SUV with blacked-out windows roared up. She immediately looked to Dash. He nodded as he thanked the tow truck driver, who promised to have the vehicle fixed up and delivered home by breakfast. The SUV driver walked up to Dash before handing over keys.

"Your rental, sir," the man said.

"Thank you." Dash took the offering. The guy hopped into the tow truck with a final wave.

Never had she seen—or would get used to—the kind of money Dash had at his disposal. She didn't care especially. He was down-to-earth, and half the time she was around him, she forgot how ridiculously rich he was. Until she looked around and remembered how much his apartment or the vehicles he drove must have cost.

He ushered her into the passenger seat of the SUV as the creepy feeling of eyes watching crept over her. She shivered involuntarily at the thought someone so cunning was out there.

"I'm definitely not letting you out of my sight now." Dash's words, his voice, sent warmth rocketing through her. She knew better than to let herself get used to them.

"Tell her the truth. We're not a couple," she said, trying to keep emotion out of her tone. It had been a day for the books. She'd visited her best friend in jail. She'd almost been shot. She'd confronted Sheldon. And now this. Her mind snapped to the heated kisses in her bedroom, but she forced those suckers out of her mind as fast as she could. It wouldn't do any good to dwell on the fact that Dash was the best kisser she'd ever known. Or that the reality of being in his arms made her feel a kind of safety she never knew she craved.

"I would if she would believe me." Those words were the equivalent of a half dozen bee stings.

"Then make her. Call her out. I can't go around watching my back every five seconds and I won't." Anger and fear were a potent mix. Both were stalking her.

"I'm sorry."

"Why? She's the crazy one," she quickly countered.

"True. But it's my fault she is targeting you. And she won't believe we're not together. Now, you're in more danger and—"

"I chose to be here for my friend," she said, cutting him off. There was no use feeling sorry for her. She was letting off some steam and exploring options, if there were any. She didn't need his pity.

"True." There was no denying she was there of her own free will, and she was relieved he didn't try to take all the blame. "I still see it as my job to protect you, Raina."

"Why? You made it clear where we stand." She was baiting the bull out of her own fit of anger.

"Not because I don't care about you." He said the words low and under his breath to the point she barely heard them.

The reality of how dangerous his job was struck like a physical blow. His feelings didn't matter when she would never allow herself to go there anyway. Losing her father to a dangerous job had knocked the wind out of her in her young life. He'd been in love with her mother. They'd made plans. Her mother had been ordering small bags of sand off the internet to surprise him with the trip she had planned for the three of them to celebrate his last day in the military. He'd been planning on serving three years and then taking a civilian job to be there for both of them.

Through no fault of his own, he couldn't be there to take care of his wife during the most challenging time of her life. Raina didn't regret the sacrifices she made for a mother she desperately loved. But it nearly broke her heart when her mother called out her husband's name in her sleep like he'd just walked through the door.

They were supposed to have a long life together, not this.

A surprising tear broke loose from Raina's eye and rolled down her cheek. This was exactly the reason she couldn't let her heart have its way, no matter how perfect Dashiell West might be. Plus, there was Layla to consider. She wouldn't like a relationship between her best friend and her brother after she'd worked so hard to carve her own way in life. If that wasn't enough, there was Dash. He'd been clear. He didn't do long term. Period.

Chapter Fifteen

Dash studied his cell phone at a red light.

"What is it?" Raina asked. "What's wrong?"

"Liam just sent over an interesting piece of intel about Alec Kingsley," Dash said. "Turns out, he was bullied as a kid."

"Don't take this the wrong way, but a lot of people were because most aren't your size," she said.

"Fair enough. Alec was bullied in the small prep school he attended," he continued. "He was captain of the chess club and started a kids-in-tech club at school. Alec knows quite a bit about computer programming."

"That is interesting. And confusing. Wouldn't he take more than two million dollars if he could?" she asked.

"You would think so. He might have seen low-hanging fruit with my sister and decided to test the waters," he said. "Plus, according to HR, he was on his way out. A few of his bigger clients were complaining about him."

"What were the complaints about?" she asked.

"He was losing money, missing opportunities and not being responsive when they called," he said.

"That would be devastating to a career where relationships are everything." She bit down on her bottom lip. "Speaking of relationships, where are we on Calum's wife? And where are we going? This isn't the way to your place."

Dash glanced back at his phone. "She's our next stop. They live in a one-point-five-million-dollar town house in the Laurelhurst area."

"I know where that is," she said. "North of Washington Park Arboretum near the University District. It's a high-rent area."

"That's a lot of money for a town house," he concurred. "Especially one with only two bedrooms."

"It'd be easy to lock and go. I bet they have another place on one of the islands," she pointed out.

"A quick escape."

She exhaled. "From everything I've heard, kids change everything. It wouldn't surprise me to learn they were putting their town house on the market. Some people move to Bainbridge as their main address and then keep an apartment in Seattle for those long work nights."

He nodded.

"What's her name?" Raina asked.

"Penelope, but she goes by the name Bitty. Apparently, her mom called her Itty Bitty, and the last part stuck," he supplied. At least some of the research was bearing fruit.

"What do you think about Sheldon? Innocent or guilty?" she asked point-blank.

"We know he's guilty of hacking into the system. Did he take the money?" He paused for a couple of beats. "I'm not sure. We'll have the team dig into his financials. We have his signature down, and that could help us connect him to the money on the back end."

"The company might not want to press charges," she stated. "I found a glitch in the system that was causing clients to be overbilled once. I reported it to my manager, who got all excited. The executives ended up making me sign an additional nondisclosure agreement about the finding, and they just had us quietly fix the bug."

"No one wants the bad press, especially when it comes to a financial mistake for a financial company." There were so many reasons he'd left corporate America, and that was high on the list. There was so much inefficiency and too much padding CEOs' salaries. Too much politics. He couldn't deal with it on a day-to-day basis, so he'd developed an exit strategy that had more than worked out for him.

Dash pulled into the town house complex and stopped in front of unit 30.

"What do we know about Bitty?" Raina nodded toward the town house. As she walked past Dash, she muttered, "And I'm guessing Stuart is now so far down the list we don't need to worry about swinging by his place."

Dash nodded before continuing, "Graduated from

a highly regarded prep school in California. Met Calum in college at a frat party. She splits her time between Junior League and volunteering at the museum. Her parents live in LA, where she grew up, and she's an only child."

"Smart?" she asked.

"Got through college with a 3.8 grade point average," he informed her, skimming more of the file on his phone.

"Not exactly a slouch."

"No." He read toward the bottom. "Interior design major. Works part-time for her father's real estate business."

"Keeping it in the family," she said as she took the couple of steps to the porch.

"Seems like it."

The twin double doors were flanked by brightly colored potted flowers. There was a decorative wrought-iron bench to Dash's right. He knocked on the door.

"Coming," came a cheerful voice from inside. Bitty sounded like she was expecting someone.

The door opened with a whoosh, and a very elegant, slick-haired blonde stood there. Her face went from open and smiling to confused. "I'm sorry." She stepped toward them and closed the door around her. "Can I help you with something?"

Dash flashed his badge as her gaze bounced from him to Raina to the waiting SUV and back. "Special Agent Dash West, and this is my friend Raina. We'd like to ask you a few questions if you can spare a moment of your time."

"Is this about the security breach at the firm?" She raised one carefully manicured eyebrow.

"Yes." In a manner of speaking, it was. There was a whole lot more to the story, but Dash didn't figure this was the time to show his hand. "Could we come in?"

"Sure." She opened the door wider and took a step back. "My husband already left for work, and my assistant will be here any minute." She dropped her hand down to her belly, and Dash wondered if she had done it subconsciously or not. "We're working on a design for the baby's room."

"Congratulations," Dash said. He'd always gotten further with witnesses by being polite, despite what those cop shows showed on TV. And the BAU worked with local law enforcement agencies, not against them.

"Thank you." She took them into the kitchen. "You're welcome to sit." She motioned toward a pair of bar chairs tucked underneath a white granite island. The counter was rounded on one side where the chairs were.

"What can you tell me about the breach?" Dash's question caused a frown.

She threw her hands up. "I don't know that much about my husband's work environment. We have a strict rule that all thoughts and conversations about work stay on the other side of that door."

"I understand." Dash took a seat. "Sounds like a good policy too."

"Are you married?" she asked.

"Me? No, ma'am."

"Please, call me Bitty. Everyone does." She wore all white. Her clothes were fitted, and there was no sign of the pregnancy yet.

"Speaking of marriages, how have you and Mr. Langston been getting along?" Dash asked.

Her eyebrows drew together. "I'm confused. What does my marriage have to do with the breach in security at my…" It seemed to dawn on her that family members could be viewed as suspects. "Oh. Are you asking if my marriage is solid?"

"Yes, ma'am. I apologize for the personal nature of the question."

She nodded and took in a deep breath. "I'd say we have a good marriage."

Under the counter and out of view, Dash saw Raina's hands clench as they sat on top of her thighs.

"Again, excuse the personal nature of my questions. It's the hard part of my line of work," he said in a calm voice that begged forgiveness. "I wouldn't be doing my job if I didn't ask."

"Of course. Go on. I'll answer anything I can. I'd like to help." Her blonde hair was a dye job, but he wouldn't know it from the roots. It didn't match her dark brown eyebrows, despite being otherwise meticulously maintained. In fact, everything about her was put together perfectly from the outside.

The house was immaculate. It looked like some-

thing off one of those home renovation shows before anyone actually lived in it, down to the bowl of
limes perfectly situated on the counter. There were
no visible snacks sitting out. Not a single chip bag.

"Is your husband faithful in your marriage?" he
asked.

A storm brewed behind her paper bag–brown
eyes. Her hand went to her belly. Again, he wondered if she even realized she'd made the move or
if it was some kind of subconscious maternal reaction. He'd seen it with other witnesses and suspects.

The image of Raina pregnant with his child
snapped into his thoughts, catching him off guard.
Dash didn't even want kids, so his mind was definitely playing tricks on him.

He also thought about Bitty's cheating husband
and the fact that this man manipulated the sister he'd
sworn to protect. Relationships held in secrecy were
never good for one of the parties. The memory of
how his sister had looked in chains slammed into
him. Despite her tough exterior, she'd never looked
more lost and alone to him.

Bitty straightened her back, and a sour look
passed over her features. She looked at Raina. "What
did you say your name was again?"

"I'M RAINA."

Calum's wife shot a death stare at Raina as though
she was the one who'd had an affair with the woman's husband.

"Do you work for the government?" Bitty asked.

"No, ma'am. I work at the same place your husband does."

Bitty went from innocent-looking, newly pregnant housewife to talons-out witch-face in two seconds. Raina had never seen a person transform so quickly. She'd been sizing Bitty up to see if she believed the woman was capable of outsmarting Layla. It would take a certain degree of intelligence to pull off hacking into the system. Bitty would have potentially had access to Layla's computer at work if she ever accompanied her husband to the office.

"Is there anything else you'd like to ask?" Bitty turned her attention to Dash as though Raina had left the room. The chill in the air was marked, and agitation was written all over her face.

"You haven't answered my last question yet," Dash persisted.

"I think that's too personal, and I'm going to have to ask you to leave," she said.

"We can do this here where you're comfortable or I can bring you in for questioning. Either way, you're going to have to answer. Unless you don't want to cooperate anymore." Dash had just the right mix of calm and inquisitive. The man was brilliant, and Raina had no idea how he could quash his personal feelings so well and keep a straight face. He had to be seething inside as much as she was.

Normally, she would feel sorry for someone whose husband cheated on them, but there was something about Bitty that left an uneasy feeling in the pit of Raina's stomach. She couldn't pinpoint the feeling exactly.

"Calum was…tempted by someone at work. A young woman who threw herself at my husband. He gave in to temptation, but that's long over now. We've moved on and are planning our family." She folded her arms over her chest. "Now, if there are no more questions, I'd like for you to leave."

Dash stood up, thanked her and walked out the front door with Raina. It wasn't until they were inside the vehicle that he let down the facade. There was pure rage in his eyes. "I can't wait to hear what Calum Langston has to say about the affair."

"He knows I'm close with Layla. I doubt he'd try to lie in front of me." And just as they were about to leave, Calum pulled up in his Range Rover.

Chapter Sixteen

Dash should probably walk away from this one and let one of his colleagues handle the interview. Pulling on all his strength, he turned to Raina. "It might be best if you stay in the vehicle while I ask him a few questions. I want to hear his version of events if he thinks he can get away with lying."

She nodded, and she didn't debate his actions when he leaned over and kissed her.

Dash only had a few seconds after Calum pulled into his garage to catch him before his wife did. Dash would bet she was too angry to call him, and she probably knew he was on his way home anyway. Some conversations went down better in person, and she seemed the type to want to watch her husband squirm.

Her sweet, innocent housewife routine had morphed quickly once Dash started asking the hard questions. He wanted to grab Calum before the garage door closed, so Dash hopped out of the back seat.

"Excuse me, sir." He waved his hands in the air so

Calum could see them. Facing the man who used his baby sister was going to take all the strength he could muster. He kept his cool by reminding himself this was the best way to get Layla out of the trouble she was in. Get Calum talking and he could figure out his level of involvement. Bitty had climbed up a few notches on the suspect list after their conversation.

Calum hopped out of the driver's side of his vehicle, looking sweaty and wearing workout clothes. He had that sandy-blond California look, despite originally being from Arizona. He looked Dash up and down, his gaze focusing on Dash's holster. "Can I help you?"

"I'd like to ask a few questions, if I may. My name is Special Agent Dash West and I work for the FBI." Dash didn't have the right to enter Calum's garage without permission. "May I?"

Calum stood in an athletic stance, feet about hip-width apart, arms crossed over his chest. "Not until I know what this is about."

This conversation wasn't starting off well. Dash figured he might as well go for broke. "I want to talk to you about your affair with someone in your office."

Calum raked his fingers through his perfect hair. "Damn, not this. My wife has already had enough. She'll leave me."

There was a desperate quality to his tone that surprised Dash.

"Layla West is sitting in prison right now. Whether or not your wife leaves you doesn't stack up to what has happened to her, does it?" Dash couldn't help himself. His brotherly instincts took over. He fisted his hands at his sides and, by sheer force of will, stopped himself from plowing into the jerk.

"Hey, man. I didn't have anything to do with her ripping off the company." He put his hands in the air in the surrender position. "That, she did all on her own."

"You spent time with her. Do you really think she's capable of stealing from the company?" Dash fired off.

"Capable? She's one of the smartest people I've ever met. Yes, she's more than capable. Would she do something like this and implicate herself? No way. Layla's too smart for that," he said.

"Then you believe she was set up?" Dash pressed.

"I don't know what to believe anymore. All I do know is that if I don't get my butt inside the house, my wife is going to have a fit. I've already put her through the wringer. I'm on my third strike. So, if you don't mind…"

"Don't go anywhere out of town in case I or someone from the Behavioral Analysis Unit needs to get in touch with you," Dash stated. Yes, he was seething. And yes, it was taking all his willpower to keep his feet planted and not deck Calum Langston. The guy was a jerk, but based on his answers and his actions, Dash didn't believe he'd set up Layla. The timing of their affair was unfortunate for him because it was going to be public knowledge if it wasn't already.

Revenge was a strong motive. Hurting his mistress and teaching him a lesson in the process. Was Bitty that calculating?

Dash climbed in the SUV. "We're going to my sister's apartment."

Raina shot him a confused look.

"I haven't been by there in the past week since her arrest. I want to dig around the place and see if we can pick up any clues," he said.

"We should probably eat something," Raina said, and he realized they hadn't eaten breakfast yet. "It doesn't have to be much. I can get by on power bars when I'm coding."

"We can do a little better than that," he said, wanting to share his favorite breakfast burrito spot. "This place is on the way to Layla's."

It was most likely the stress of the day combined with the pull of attraction he hadn't felt in far too long before Raina that had him wanting…no, *needing* to reach over and kiss her again.

Not the time, West. Not the time.

LAYLA'S DOWNTOWN APARTMENT was pristine, like always. Raina had no idea what they were looking for, and going inside the place without her friend felt like trespassing. "What are we trying to find?"

"Good question." Dash stood in the middle of the living room and glanced around, surveying the area.

The flooring inside the apartment was wood, stained in a light color. The furniture was all white, and there was a painting of a red dot over the fireplace that Raina would never understand the price tag of.

"Nothing looks out of sorts," she said. Nothing was ever out of place.

Two small sofas faced each other. Each had a red throw blanket folded over the back. The cleaning lady who came in every week made sure everything stayed in its appropriate spot. Layla worked long hours, so she wasn't home much.

Dash moved to the kitchen. Again, there was nothing to find there. Layla didn't cook, despite having all brand-new stainless steel appliances and a gas cooktop. Raina had only ever seen her friend use the microwave on a regular basis. Not unusual for a young, single professional woman.

He opened the fridge. There were a few takeout boxes and a carton of milk. There were a couple of yogurts—Layla's go-to breakfast—and some once-fresh fruit that looked pitiful. He tossed it and the stale takeout containers. Other than that, there was orange juice and a couple bottles of wine. He picked one up and read the label.

"Expensive," he said low and under his breath. He of all people should know Layla had a thirst for the good life. It was half the reason she worked her behind off.

There was a wet bar in the hallway leading to the living room. Raina took him by the hand and walked him over. She opened the pocket doors that revealed the expensive stuff.

"I don't even drink this on a regular basis." He

picked up one of a dozen bottles of champagne to the tune of two hundred plus dollars each.

Raina shrugged. "What can I say? Your sister has expensive taste."

Looking at it from his perspective, he had to be thinking this wouldn't look good to a jury. A young ex-criminal who'd used her computer skills to wash her background clean and then go to work at a financial company, where she got greedy and made two million dollars disappear.

It was a sound bite that would sell. It was clickbait that would work. No one bothered to dig deeper and find the truth. Most people seemed to make up their mind after the ten- or fifteen-second pitch. It didn't help that there'd been an attempt to cover the tracks on the password that had been used.

Anyone who knew Layla would realize she wouldn't be that sloppy. But Raina, Dash and even Calum weren't the ones who would be picked to decide her fate.

There was something about Sheldon that still wasn't sitting right with Raina, though. She couldn't quite pinpoint it. He was angry with everyone. Did he have a beef with Layla? Revenge would be a good motive. But, also, just proving that he could do it might be enough for him to feel like he was getting one over on everyone. She had no idea people were making Sheldon's life so hard. It shouldn't surprise her, though. Layla's boss also still bothered Raina. It was news to her that clients were complaining about him. But then, working in another department would mean that she wouldn't necessarily get word. Heck, she didn't know what was going on with her own team half the time. Then there was Bitty. Raina didn't trust that woman as far as she could throw her. A spoiled LA princess whose husband cheated on her… Raina didn't see Bitty taking that lying down. She had admitted to knowing about the affair. She didn't need the money. Two million dollars would be enough to have Layla locked up for a long time. What lengths would she go to keep her family intact?

Then there was Talia to consider. How far would she go? The black rose on the seat was more than a threat. It was also her telling them both she could get to either one of them at any point in time if she wanted to.

The motorcycle guy was serious. He had tried to shoot at Dash and probably her, as well. He would have run them off the road. He'd been going after them. Why? Who was he working for?

Talia was a possibility despite Dash thinking she wouldn't put him at risk. He hadn't seen her in two years. She'd been out for six months, circling like a vulture.

Raina's cell phone buzzed. She'd been so deep in thought the noise made her jump.

She fished her cell out of her handbag and checked the screen. Her landlord. She must have made a face, because Dash asked, "Is everything okay?"

"I'll let you know in a sec." Her landlord rarely ever called. She answered on the second ring. "Hello?"

"Where are you?" Mrs. Applebaum's voice wasn't right.

"I'm in Seattle. Why? Is everything okay?"

"Thank the stars you're not home." The relief in her voice was palpable. "I saw your bike in the garage and your car was here, so I assumed the worst. I drove my husband up the wall, and he suggested that I call you."

"Why? What has you so worried?"

"Your apartment, dear. Something caught on fire. The firemen are here now, putting out the blaze, but I was so worried you were inside," she said.

"My house is on fire?"

"Yes. I'm sorry to be the one to tell you, but I was worried sick," her landlord continued. "Don't you worry—we'll get insurance right on it. The blaze moved so fast I don't know how."

Raina sat down on the edge of Layla's bed. She was momentarily stunned. "Have the firemen determined the cause?"

"They haven't said anything yet. We ran across the street in case it jumped to the main house. It didn't, so our place is safe, and you're welcome to stay in the spare bedroom until we can sort out the insurance and rebuild. Of course, you can break your lease without penalty too. You let me know what you decide once you figure out what's left and where you want to go." Her landlords had always been kind and fair, so it didn't surprise her that they were willing to rush to take full responsibility.

She feared the fire was no accident. *Talia?*

"Thank you for calling and letting me know, Mrs. Applebaum. Can I ask how bad the fire was?"

"It covered the place fast. So fast. I'm not sure much will be salvageable," she said after a sigh.

"I'll come home right now and—"

"There isn't much to see here. Of course, you're welcome to come back if you want, but the police are cordoning off the entrance," she informed her. "It looks like it took pretty much the whole second floor over the garage."

"Oh. Okay, well, thank you anyway. I'll check in later. I have a place to stay tonight. In fact, I was planning to be away from home for a few days anyway. Would you mind keeping me posted and letting me know what survives?" Raina asked as dread settled over her. She didn't have much, but the thought of losing what little she had caused a heavy weight to settle on her shoulders like a cold, wet blanket.

"I will do that as soon as the firemen give me a report. I'll be honest, it doesn't look like much, if anything, made it. I'm sorry this happened." Mrs. Applebaum meant it too. She was exactly the kind of person who would care more about Raina's feelings and safety than her rent or the loss. "I'm just real glad you weren't home."

"Thank you. Same here." Raina ended the call and put her head in her hands. "It's all gone."

"What is gone?" Dash came to her side and sat down next to her. The mattress dipped under his weight.

"Everything. My dad's medals. My mom's favorite necklace. Things I can't replace." Raina was not a crier. *So* not a crier. But this made her want to bawl.

No. Whoever did this didn't get to win. The person could take away her possessions, but she still had her memories—memories that she would cherish for the rest of her life.

"How? What happened, Raina?" He cupped her chin and tilted her face toward him. A rogue tear slipped out that he thumbed away.

"A fire in my apartment."

"Talia," he said under his breath. He fished his cell from his pocket and fired off a text, presumably to one of his colleagues.

"Could be someone who is not very happy with me being part of this investigation," she said.

"Not likely," he countered.

"Why not?" She was actually curious about his response. Her life had been pretty straightforward—albeit a little bit boring—before all this…mess had started with Layla. Maybe someone was trying to silence her too.

"Well, first of all, Talia is the only one who would have something against you personally. This fire… this is a very personal attack. It doesn't match up with the other case," he said.

"Someone tried to kill me as much as they tried to kill you," she reasoned.

"True. The jury is still out on who was responsible for the attack," he said. "But I've all but dismissed Talia, considering the fact she wouldn't want to have me killed. She wants me to suffer and come back to her, begging her forgiveness. The psych profile doesn't match up."

"Unless she changed her mind while she was locked up." Stranger things had happened. "Layla's case is still so confusing. We have a few suspects, but I don't have a front-runner. I don't feel closer to the truth than we were twenty-four hours ago."

"It's been a long morning. Neither of us slept last night." His voice was smooth like silk now, and that's exactly how it felt as it washed over her.

"This day barely started and it feels like it might never end."

"I'll keep looking around my sister's place. Why don't you take a shower? There's no reason we can't plant here for the day," he said.

"I can name one. I left my laptop at your place." She bit back a yawn. Lack of sleep was clearly taking its toll. She never went anywhere without her laptop but leaving it at Dash's place was safer than taking it with her under the circumstances.

"True." He stood up and held his hands out.

She placed her hands in his and felt the jolt of electricity all the way up her arms.

"But the brain starts slowing down after so many hours trying to figure something out. It's natural to need sleep. You've been in these clothes since yesterday morning, and it might help you think if you take a hot shower and change." His grin was devastating to her heart. "I'll do my best not to think of you naked in the next room."

She used him as leverage to pull herself up to standing. "Is that right?"

"I think we both know the two of us being together wouldn't work for more reasons than we care to count. My heart has yet to get the memo," he admitted, and there was something irresistible about his honesty.

Should she fight what felt like the most natural thing in the world? Or would another hot kiss douse some of the flames still flickering between them?

Chapter Seventeen

Dash couldn't help but think about how small Raina's hands were in comparison to his. Her creamy skin was like silk against his palms as he walked her the couple of steps to the master bedroom.

He wasn't kidding about the fact that it had been a long twenty-four hours. Adrenaline had spiked several times and was now depleted, leaving Raina with the wired-tired feeling he could so easily see in her eyes.

She needed rest. Continuing to operate with an empty tank would yield a similar result as driving a car on E. Convincing her to take time away from the investigation was a whole different ball game. But he could start with a shower and a fresh change of clothes. She and his sister couldn't be too far off in clothing size, and Layla had to have something casual that would fit Raina. Of course, general height and weight was where the similarities between the two ended.

Raina was nothing like Layla physically, mentally or emotionally.

It was easy to see why the two were friends. They were opposites in most every way. Layla lived in an expensive apartment as close to the action as possible, whereas Raina lived over someone's garage on an island. She rode a bike, which was something Layla wouldn't be caught dead doing. Layla drove an expensive sports car. Looking around her apartment cemented the idea that his sister preferred the finer things in life.

Was she hiding something? He hated to think about her in those terms, and he didn't believe she was guilty by any means, but her attorney was going to have to sell her innocence in a court of law if Dash didn't nail the bastard who was actually responsible for this.

Another thought occurred to him. Was she protecting someone?

"Was there anyone else in Layla's life?" he asked Raina as he pulled a fluffy chocolate-brown towel from the hall closet. He set it on top of the counter and then headed toward the door.

"Since Calum?"

"In addition to?" he asked.

"No. At least, I don't think so," she said. "But then, she didn't tell me about Calum until long into the relationship. I seriously doubt there would have been anyone else. She was pretty into him. And, to be fair, I suspected something was up at the time when she started canceling plans with me and it took her a long time to answer a text. I just didn't know who she was seeing."

Dash let that sit as he exited the bathroom. He closed the door behind him to give Raina some privacy. He wasn't worried about her finding fresh clothes. As close as she was to his sister, Raina most likely had left something behind. And if she didn't, his sister wouldn't mind if her best friend borrowed an outfit. Layla faced bigger battles at the present time.

He forced his thoughts away from the kisses he and Raina had shared, despite them wanting to force their way into his mind and take center stage. The attraction simmering between them wasn't something he'd experienced in the past but it had gone as far as they could allow.

Speaking of fires, the one at her place bothered him more than he was letting on. He had half a mind to reach out to Talia and give her hell about it. But that would be the equivalent of pouring gasoline on a blaze and definitely fell into the category of counterproductive.

It also required an update to his team, which he gave almost immediately. Looking around, he spotted Layla's laptop on top of her bar-height counter that separated the living room from the kitchen. He booted up her system figuring he could give the password she provided a go.

He set up his cell phone, using the wall-mounted flat-screen TV as a monitor.

Every day for at least fifteen minutes, Dash needed to sit in as quiet a room as possible and process the events. On a run like this one going on no sleep, it was especially important. He never knew when one little detail would suddenly pop and click the puzzle pieces of an investigation together. While Raina finished up her shower, he turned the lights down and leaned back into the couch.

He closed his eyes and reviewed, beginning with yesterday morning's meeting with the team. From there, he went to Layla's office to interview Alec Kingsley. In all the excitement of the day, Dash almost forgot about the video he'd taken of Kingsley with the mystery man. He made a mental note to review the video and check in with home base as to whether or not the guy had been identified.

Raina hadn't recognized him, which led Dash to believe the guy was an outsider to the firm. A client? A rival company? To be fair, he could be a consultant. As much as technology had sped up investigations, this one couldn't move fast enough for Dash.

Layla's boss had been distressed in the meeting. Nervous? Then there was the fact that the guy was unhappy at work.

Sheldon was an interesting character. He had the ability to steal from the company. He had the motivation. It would be the perfect 'up yours' to an organization that hadn't been all that kind to him. He'd gotten out. If the signature fit or they could locate the money, Sheldon was going down. Dash didn't like Sheldon. He didn't trust the kid. Did he steal two million dollars?

There was nothing about Calum Langston that Dash liked. Number one offense…the married man with a pregnant wife had had an affair with Layla by deceiving her about his personal situation. Layla was smart, but she wasn't experienced in love. She was still young and her heart was still tender despite the steel facade. She put up a good front but underneath it all, she still had a lot to learn. What was it about smart women and bad choices in men?

Calum would be considered good looking by most standards—there was that. Dash was certain the guy could be charming. His lines? Those were tired. Of course he was "in the process of divorcing his wife." An experienced person would see that for the load of bull it was. Someone who was young and naive when it came to the heart would take the bait.

Dash didn't like Calum, but he highly doubted the man had set Layla up. He did, however, seem under the thumb of an ice-queen wife. Bitty had sent all kinds of warning flares up. She had motive: revenge. She could be punishing both her husband for his affair and his mistress for having the audacity to try to take her husband from her. Bitty was high on the suspect list. Could Calum have been an accomplice to prove his love to his wife? Could he have been the one to set Layla up? Both were possibilities. Dash wouldn't rule Calum out on that basis.

The motorcycle proved a professional was involved. Who would have those kinds of connections? Not a typical VP in a financial firm. The more he thought about it, he couldn't ignore Talia as a possibility.

Alec? He was connected to organized crime,

based on the pictures in his office. He was dissatis-
fied at work and seemed to have a lot of heat about
his job performance coming down on him. But why
target Layla? By all accounts, she got along with her
boss. There didn't seem to be any friction there. Had
he accidentally come across her password? Installed
something on her computer to record her keystrokes?

Anyone inside the office would have access to
her computer.

Talia. Would she target his baby sister to get back
at him? The short answer was a resounding yes. Did
he think she was responsible for this crime? No. Not
really, though he couldn't pinpoint an exact reason.
He was relying on good old-fashioned instinct there.
His gut said she wasn't responsible for motorcycle man. Again, she wanted Dash to suffer, and he
couldn't do that if he was dead.

Motorcycle man could be the response to Dash
spending the day stirring up the pot. A warning to
back off.

An attack on a federal officer wasn't a person's
best move. The perp must be awfully confident the
crime couldn't be tied back to him or her.

Then there was the fire. A warning? Talia might
actually be responsible there. She would want to send
a warning to Raina to leave Dash alone. Talia's last
words to Dash involved a threat to anyone he dated.
Eventually, she would let it all go and move on. Except that she'd only been out for six months after
serving a year and a half of a two year sentence.
Dash was fresh on her mind.

Since Talia had been circling his place, she had to have seen him with Raina. Talia had to be behind the fire. Linking her to arson was a whole different story. Could he confront her? Make her see there was no hope of getting back together? Could he convince her to move on? Now that she was out of prison, didn't she want to keep her freedom?

Or had she moved on and now wanted revenge? Eighteen months was a long time to sit behind bars.

Being beautiful wasn't Talia's problem. Being smart wasn't Talia's problem. Talia's problem was nonnegotiable in a relationship: honesty.

Dash couldn't be with someone who wasn't honest. It just wouldn't work. In fact, lately, he could only see himself with someone like Raina.

RAINA CLEARED HER THROAT before entering the living room. She didn't want to surprise a man who kept a gun at the ready.

"Hey." He opened his eyes slowly in the dimly lit room.

Somehow, she didn't think she'd caught him off guard. Then again, a person in his line of work would be cued up for any sound. His reflexes were ridiculous. Don't even get her started on the bod that proved gym memberships were definitely worth the time and energy. The word *sculpted* came to mind. There were a few others, but all would be entering dangerous turf if she let herself dwell on them.

She could see herself with Dash. *Really* see herself with him. But could she get past his dangerous job? A job that meant he might not come home for supper at night. Or ever. The possibility of being left alone like her mother was a lot to think about.

It was probably a good thing Dash would never let it get that far between them. He was the king of maintaining control.

"Mind if I join you? I didn't want to disturb you." She stood there in the oversized T-shirt and leggings, thinking about how thin the material was.

"Yes." He pushed up to sitting in a straighter position and rubbed his eyes with the heels of his hands.

She walked over to the sofa and sat down on one end, biting back a yawn.

Dash reached for her hand and then tugged her closer. "It's okay. I promise I won't bite."

"I wasn't worried about being bitten." She was, however, concerned about the heat in the kisses they'd shared. She'd never known passion that could ignite so quickly or burn so intensely. So, yeah, she was a little freaked out by it and a lot intrigued. If he was anyone else, she'd be all in to explore just how that changed a relationship. Again, his job made him off-limits as much as his family connection did.

He smiled that devastating smile of his.

"What have you worked out so far?" She knew he was sitting here thinking about the case.

He briefed her on his thoughts. They were a similar view to hers. She told him about her parents and was suddenly interested in learning more about his. "Tell me about your family. Aside from your sister."

"We had great parents. Our dad spent his career at Portland PD after relocating from Texas," he started.

"I didn't know that." She didn't bother to hide the shock in her voice.

"Layla didn't tell you?" He seemed just as surprised.

"No. She said it was a sad story and she didn't want to. I never forced her, figuring she would whenever she was ready. The day never came," she admitted.

"Dad was much older by the time she was born. He worked a lot of the time, and I think he lost himself in his job after Mom died," he said. "Our father raised us to prize honesty and integrity and fight injustice." He rubbed the scruff on his chin. "He was the anticorruption leader in the PD. I had both parents growing up. Layla had Dad after Mom died. Layla was young too. I should have stopped by more often. I never thought about how lonely she might be. That pretty much makes me a jerk."

"I think it makes you human. You had your own life. She had your father," she said. "She did mention something about a babysitter. Said it was a dark time in her life and refused to talk about it beyond that. She hated the color purple because of it."

"Hmm. That's news to me. She never said anything about having a rough time with a sitter. But she did say her friend used to force a blindfold on her that was a purple bandana while the friend had a guy over when they were younger." His eyebrows drew together. It was easy to see how much he cared about his baby sister and how hard he was taking the revelation. His eyes took on that storm-like quality. His expression became serious when he talked about the past. "I didn't realize how tough she took our mom's death. I think our dad was mourning so hard he probably wasn't paying as much attention to Layla as he could have been. I can't fault the man for loving his wife. Did Layla ever tell you she was the one driving the car when it crashed?"

"Oh no." Raina's heart clenched.

"I'm guessing she didn't share that piece of news," he said on a sigh. "Not her fault but she doesn't see it that way."

"I'm so sorry. Do you mind if I ask how your mother died?" Her mind immediately snapped to his mother working in law enforcement or some type of high-risk job.

"Antibiotic allergy. We were eating out for some special reason… I can't even remember, or maybe I blocked it out. And she ate a bite of duck. Apparently, duck is injected with all kinds of antibiotics. Or, at least, that one was. Anyway, we didn't know about the allergy. The antibiotic isn't widely used. She went into anaphylactic shock and was pronounced dead at the hospital." There was such a sad quality to his voice.

"I know it happened a long time ago, Dash, but I'm so sorry. That's tragic and so unexpected." Raina thought about that for a minute. How random—eating out one minute and having an extreme allergic reaction to something they didn't even know was in the food. How awful.

"Thank you. It means a lot coming from you."

Raina had to force her gaze away from those gorgeous, tormented eyes of his. She took in a slow breath but only ended up ushering in more of his spicy male scent. She had to fist her hands to stop herself from reaching out to him. "It's terrible. And she was so young."

When she really thought about it, life held no guarantees. She never could have predicted a fire at her home. She never could have predicted surviving the motorcycle man. There was no way she could have predicted her best friend ending up in prison for a crime she didn't commit or the fact that Raina was here with Dash at exactly this moment in time.

Holding back and not experiencing life for fear of losing someone seemed a little misguided to her now. Dash was incredibly sexy when he was vulnerable— a rare moment with a person like him. And, yes, he had a dangerous job but he was also very good at it.

So, this time, she climbed in Dash's lap and initiated a kiss.

"I'm sorry." Her mouth moved against his as she spoke.

He didn't respond with words. Instead, he placed his hands on the small of her back as she looped hers around his neck. The move brought her breasts flush with his muscled chest, and he was like touching a brick wall. Silk over steel, she remembered.

Maybe it was from needing a release valve for

the tension of the day, but their breaths quickened as she drove her tongue inside his mouth. Her fingers traced the rigid lines of his shoulders and arms as he splayed his hands on her back, urging her toward him.

She nipped at his bottom lip and tugged it in between her teeth.

Her actions spurred him on, and he picked her up and then spun her around on her back so fast. She wrapped her legs around his midsection in an attempt to hold on. She could feel him at the V between her legs, and she craved more.

Giving in to the moment was fine. Anything more and she wouldn't be able to walk away from him. One night would never be enough with Dash West, and she didn't do short term anyway.

He seemed to be running on the same track when he pushed up off the couch. He locked gazes with her. "I want this more than I've wanted to be with anyone else in my life. When we make love, I want to take my sweet time. Right now, we both have other priorities that need our full attention, and I don't want any distractions."

The fact that he'd said *when* and not *if* sent her stomach free-falling again as a sense of anticipation settled in.

Chapter Eighteen

"I wish we were the ones setting up at Sheldon's house to watch him." Dash didn't mind surveillance, except for the part about not being able to use a proper bathroom for hours on end. It was boring work to many, but he caught so many little things with personal observation that might otherwise go unnoticed he'd come to appreciate the value of it.

Without a warrant, he couldn't legally bug Sheldon's apartment—or Calum's town house, for that matter. Would there be vans outside with listening devices homed in to each place? That was a hard yes.

There were ways around those. Anyone smart enough to steal two million dollars from an investment firm would realize they needed to stay on the down-low after receiving a visit from a federal agent.

"Leaving here doesn't seem like a smart move after what we've been through." Raina bit back another yawn.

He grabbed the throw blanket from the back of the couch and spread it out over her. She curled up on her side with her cell phone at the ready.

"We'll head out in a couple of hours. Might be a good idea to rest your eyes for now." That was basically code for go to sleep. Dash didn't need it. He could go for days without much in the way of shut-eye. Under normal circumstances, Raina probably could too. But this was a far cry from a coding session.

Raina's eyes sprang open almost the second they closed. She pushed up to a sitting position again. "My mom."

"Where is she?" he asked.

"Island Rehab. It's a small place not too far from where I live. What if the person who is after me goes after my mom instead?" Her chin jutted out like she was determined not to cry, but it also quivered just a little. This was the place she was most vulnerable, very much like his sister was to him.

"Let's get them on the phone," he said. "I can send someone from the BAU for insurance, but I imagine they have security of their own."

Raina shot him a look. "It's loose at best. They deal with a fair amount of traumatic brain injury patients. The biggest threat is their patients getting out more so than someone coming in."

"Talia is cunning. She could walk right past the front desk. I need someone there who would know how to handle her," Dash said.

Raina got up and started pacing. She held the phone to her ear after hitting the contact. "Hi, Michelle. It's Raina." She paused for a few beats. "Yeah, sorry to hear about your aunt. I hope she feels better soon. I just want to make sure my mom is in her room and everything is okay. I had one of those bad feelings, and I would feel so much better if someone went in to check on her." Another pause for a few beats. "Yes, of course. I'll hold."

She spun around and locked gazes with Dash. The split second she allowed her vulnerability to show through nearly gutted him. She bit down on her bottom lip so hard he thought it might bleed.

Just as quickly, she returned to the call. He was already texting Liam. There. Done. Now all he needed was confirmation.

Seconds ticked by with no response.

Thanks for the address.—T

Dash knew full well that Talia was probably baiting him. She wanted him out in public and probably was hoping for access to Raina in the meantime. She'd also found a way to intercept a message, which should be impossible.

"We have to go," he said to Raina.

"You're sure my mom is okay?" she asked, and the sound of hope in her voice caused his chest to tighten.

He immediately sent out an email to his group with the address and a signal for all hands on deck. He informed them of the breach on his phone as he hit the 'kill' app on his cell.

The response from Miguel was immediate.

We got this. Stand down on this one.

It was Dash's turn to pace as Raina ended the call after requesting no one be allowed to visit or see her mother.

"Call her back. Have her switch your mother to a new room ASAP," Dash said.

Raina's eyebrows knitted together. "Come again?"

"Ask… What was her name?"

"Michelle," she supplied.

"Call Michelle back and ask her to move your mother into a different room right now. Next door, if it's empty, but move her from where she is currently. Talia got to my phone."

At that moment, a knock pounded on the door.

Dash grabbed his weapon from the holster he'd hung on one of the high-back bar stools. He checked the peephole, and relief washed over him the minute he saw Liam.

He opened the door. In one fluid motion, he pulled Liam inside. Then, he peeked out and surveyed the hallways.

"That was quick," Dash said.

"I was in the area," Liam said.

"I know where the coffee is. Anyone else want a cup?" Raina asked.

"Yes, please," Liam said. He set his backpack down.

"Any chance you have an extra cell phone stashed in there?" Dash asked Liam before telling Raina he could make his own cup of coffee.

She immediately waved him off.

"As a matter of fact, I always carry a spare." Liam produced it.

"I figured as much." Dash motioned for Liam to take a seat on one of the sofas. "I know you can handle yourself, but I'm relieved you're safe. The unit might be in danger from my ex."

"Talia? I'll let everyone know it was her," Liam said, immediately texting the update."

"Good. Talia will always take the unexpected road," Dash said. "It's her signature."

"There is no unexpected road for me anymore. I'll always watch my back." Liam was good at his job.

Dash thought back to the end of his relationship with Talia and some of the promises, a.k.a. threats, she'd made. Everyone around him would regret it. Angry words, he'd thought. He also believed her anger would blow over at some point or that she'd move on to a different target. Dash wasn't normally wrong.

Liam handed over a new phone, one that Dash imported contacts onto from an encrypted cloud.

"Have you been making progress on the code?" Dash asked.

"Not as much as I'd like," Liam said. He issued a sharp sigh. "I'm sorry, man. Your sister doesn't deserve this."

Dash shook his head, praying his actions with Talia hadn't brought this down on her.

MAKING COFFEE GAVE Raina something to do. She would have just been pacing the floor otherwise, wearing a path in Layla's expensive rugs. The images of a fire engulfing her apartment, her best friend in jail and now her mother in jeopardy raced through her thoughts no matter how hard she tried to force them out.

There were other images that kept at her. Ones of her and her best friend's brother locked in a passionate kiss. She could still taste him. If she took in a deep breath, his spicy scent was everywhere. Kicking that image out of her head was taking a whole lot of effort.

Learning about his mother's story wasn't helping. The randomness of her death shattered all Raina's preconceived notions that taking a safe job meant a longer life. The truth was that there were no guarantees, which was scary and oddly freeing at the same time. She was beginning to realize how much losing her father had shocked her system.

Had it become easier to risk less of herself too? Stay in a "safe" zone with relationships so she didn't have to "lose" anyone? When she heard the thoughts run through her mind, she couldn't help but realize how silly it all sounded to her now. In order to protect herself from pain, she'd been stopping herself from living. Would never loving someone fully be worse than keeping her heart wrapped in Bubble Wrap and never knowing the kind of passion she felt anytime she was near Dash?

To be fair, she'd never experienced a pull so strong that her heart ached at the thought of never seeing him again. What if they decided to go down that path together? And that was a big *if*. Dash seemed just as gun shy about taking the next step as she was.

But this was an important moment anyway. Last week, she could never see herself truly opening up to another human. No one made her feel strong and beautiful in the way Dash did. No one even came close. So maybe there just hadn't been anyone in far too long who got her blood pumping hotly in her veins or made her want to push past her fears and see what the next step of a relationship might bring. She'd dated enough men to realize what she didn't want. Now, she would be willing to try for the right person.

Dwelling on this was a distraction from her bigger problems—problems like making absolutely certain her mother was safe and then thinking about the mess the fire had made.

She fixed three cups of coffee and took the first two into the living room, where Liam and Dash were studying his old phone.

"What's going on?" She set the mugs on the coffee table and dropped into a crouching position.

"We pulled up the security footage on your mother's facility," Dash supplied. He tilted the phone toward her. "Would you like to see?"

She studied the split screen. On the left was the front door to the facility. On the right was the back near the trash cans. There were two small eyes near one of the bins. The way the tiny animal slinked when it walked in the shadows made her think it was a cat. Maybe feral and in search of a meal. Poor thing.

"Miguel texted that a team would be there in a matter of minutes using a chopper. They're sending five people. One for each entrance and three to perform the actual extraction. Two of those carry your mother, if it comes down to it." The plan Dash described was well thought out.

"Can I talk to her? She isn't going to know what's going on, and she might end up scared. I hate for her to feel alone." She heard the shakiness in her own voice. What could she say? Even though she wasn't a crier, the thought of her mom feeling scared or alone had the power to bring Raina to her knees every time.

Do anything to her and she could take it. Come after her mother and that was a whole different story.

"The team will give her a shot to make her sleep. She'll wake up in a protected environment. They will work with the management to decide which staff member she has the best relationship with, and that person will accompany her until she's settled."

Wow. Just wow.

Raina was blown away. She figured Dash had something to do with ensuring her mother's comfort in addition to her safety. "I don't know how to thank you."

"You don't have to. There isn't anything I wouldn't give to have another day with either one of my folks. Consider paying it forward, but there's no debt owed with me." There was something honest and raw in his voice that made her fall a little bit deeper into him.

She reached across the coffee table and squeezed his hand. The link, although firing electricity through her fingertips, was also comforting. There was something about being in Dash's presence that had a calming effect on her, despite his kisses tilting her world on its axis.

It wouldn't be smart to get too caught up in the moment. Once this case was over, they would go back to their lives—a life she needed to pick up the pieces of now that her home was damaged. Raina had no idea how badly yet and she needed to circle back and ask. She wasn't quite ready for more bad news. Her apartment used to feel like home prior to spending time with Dash. Now, being with him felt like home.

As much as she wanted to chalk it up to the fact that he was her best friend's brother—and therefore, familiar—what she experienced with him was in an orbit of its own.

So, how was that for keeping her emotions in check?

Raina hopped up and headed back to the kitchen to the chorus of thank-yous for the mugs she'd set down. Caffeine would clear the cobwebs, yet she doubted there was a cup large enough to force Dash from her thoughts. Speaking to her mother right now was a bad idea. She would hold off on making the request until she could radiate calm.

The ceramic mug was warm against her palms as

she rolled it around before taking a sip. Something was bugging her, niggling at the back of her mind, and she couldn't figure out what it was. She went over the possible suspects again in her mind. The timing of the fire was suspect, but was it related or a casualty of her being seen with Dash?

His ex seemed intent on making certain he didn't date anyone again. She'd tried to ruin his career. She'd threatened his future relationships. It was a no-brainer she started the fire. She also complicated matters.

Talia might get in the way. She would have gotten to Raina's mother, and there was still a possibility that could happen. One that Raina couldn't put a whole lot of stock into if she wanted to keep her sanity until confirmation arrived that her mother was in safe hands.

"I have something on the monitor. The team has arrived," Dash said, as though on cue.

Raina exhaled for the first time in what felt like an hour. She joined Dash and Liam in the living room. Her nerves were shot.

"How do you guys do this on a daily basis?" she asked.

He shot her a confused look while Liam kept tapping away at the keyboard he'd set up.

"Sit around and wait for something to happen? Not know if a plan will go well or not until it might be too late?" There were half a dozen other questions that came to mind.

"I know that my actions help people when they

have had one of their worst days. I lock people up who then can't turn around and hurt someone else. There's a lot of satisfaction in my career. It's part of why I left the corporate world. I make a difference here," he explained. "To be honest, most of my cases are dealing with people I've never met. Doing this for someone I care about has me twisted up too."

Did he just say he cared about her? On some level, she knew. They just hadn't spoken much out loud except to say this couldn't happen between them. What *this* meant was anyone's guess. She knew in her heart she could never again have a casual fling with Dash, even if Layla approved—and she wouldn't. She would not want to be in the same room with them after the breakup—a breakup even she would know was imminent. Besides, she worked too hard to keep business in one box, friendship in another, and family in yet another. Mixing worlds wouldn't go over very well.

Raina's feelings ran too deep for the man, and they hadn't even gotten off the ground. So toning it down wouldn't be in the realm of possibility. She also realized she was distracting herself with this internal conversation.

Whatever had niggled at the back of her mind was back, and it was driving her crazy. She needed to figure it out because it suddenly seemed like a crucial detail to pass along to Dash and his team.

Chapter Nineteen

"Your mother is safe. No hiccups." Dash waited until confirmation had arrived before showing Raina what happened moments after the team left. He tilted his phone toward her so she could see the screen and then hit the play button on the video he'd recorded.

Raina came around the coffee table and sat next to him. She gave him a look that said she wondered if it was a good idea to watch this.

He played the video of the female figure, clad in all black, slipping through a window without alerting a soul.

"Talia?" she asked.

"Looks like it."

Raina gasped. Her hand came up to her chest. "What about the others?"

"She won't bother anyone else. She'll slip right out the minute she realizes your mother isn't there." This confirmed that Talia was behind the fire at Raina's apartment. He put the camera back on live in time to see her slip out the back door and disappear.

"Why didn't anyone stay behind to catch her?" Raina said as sirens sounded. "Is that your team?"

"Local jurisdiction." He shook his head. "She'll get away from them, though."

"My mom is safe, and she didn't bother the other residents. Those are big wins in my opinion," Raina said.

Dash fired off a text to Miguel, letting him know what had just happened with Talia and asking if anyone could be sent to do a sweep, possibly find a strand of hair or DNA left behind that could link her to the crime.

Of course, she had only slipped in and out, so technically no crime had been committed. A trespassing charge would be a stretch. It was a rehab facility, and people came and went. Unless the local law enforcement picked her up—and he highly doubted they'd be able to—getting anything to stick would be like cooking on Teflon.

"Do you want me to wipe your old phone?" Liam asked.

"I already did." Dash suddenly remembered the other video he'd taken at the café. Alec.

"I have something stored in the cloud we should take a closer look at." Dash pulled that video up. He played it a couple of times, trying to lip-read. The problem was that Alec's back was to the camera, and he was very animated. He kept glancing around, a telltale sign he was doing something he didn't want to be caught doing. "What do you make of it?"

Liam shrugged. "I can play around with it on my laptop. See if I can enhance the images."

"Take a stab. See what you can do." Dash sent the link.

"Where do we go next?" Raina asked, leaning back into the couch and massaging her temples.

"Let's stick around here, eat something and see what we can come up with on the video." He didn't want to remind her of the risk she faced now that Talia knew who she was. He also didn't want to tell her that her safest bet would be to stay right here with Liam while Dash followed up with the investigation after ordering a late lunch. He also figured she wouldn't have any of it. Raina wasn't the type to back away from perceived danger, and her loyalty to his sister was akin to the kind of bond he'd shared with the men in his unit while he was in the service and now with the BAU. After getting out of the military, he'd attained a computer science degree and had gone into a "safe" job. *Safe* in terms of finances. Having been in the service, he knew a beat cop wasn't the right job for him. As much as he loved and respected his father, Dash had known right away he wouldn't follow in the man's footsteps.

In some small way, he was honoring his father's memory by working in law enforcement. This job pulled on all his strengths, and he liked using his computer skills to solve cases. His degree gave him more tools to use…

And that got him thinking. Could he and Liam use software to lip-read? It was worth a shot. He grabbed

Layla's laptop and bypassed the operating system, pulling up Linux instead.

His fingers danced on the keyboard as she watched. She seemed to be catching on, and she offered a couple of suggestions for the program he had to write.

The only break he took was to order lunch for the three of them. At two o'clock in the afternoon, he was about to chew his arm off from hunger.

He ordered a pair of pizzas, liking the synergy they had when they combined efforts. He also liked her clean, citrusy scent filling every breath he took as he sat next to her. He wanted more. Was she forbidden fruit? Or was this real? Was it even possible to think they could…what?…go on a date after this?

That was almost laughable. They knew each other far too well for that. Hell, they'd kissed with the kind of passion that could only happen with someone he knew beyond basic greetings. It would be impossible to dial back time and start over.

Where would they start? If they could?

Pizza delivery was left in the downstairs lobby. He darted down and got back in two seconds before passing out slices.

No one seemed to want to stop working, so they ate at their respective spots.

"Bingo," she said, and there was enough pride in her voice to know that she'd finished the work well. Programmers wrote code. They tested. They never truly knew if an app was going to work the way it was intended until it went live. Then they could work out the glitches.

"Let's try it out and see what happens." He opened the video in the app they'd cowritten and studied the screen.

Nothing.

"Back to the drawing board," she said after a sigh.

They were doing something, not just sitting around watching paint dry. So that was helpful to kill the time before he headed out for a second round of interviews. He scrolled through the lines of code, looking for the mistake as Liam dozed off. No doubt, he'd been working nonstop since yesterday morning's meeting.

A thought occurred to Dash: Alec knew how to write code. Maybe they should request a sample from him. They had a sample from Sheldon already, so that was going to be easy to check against the code responsible for making millions of dollars disappear from the bank and causing his sister's arrest.

While Dash didn't exactly have a warrant to seize Alec's work computer—or home computer, for that matter—he could make a simple request. Innocent people usually cooperated with federal agents and law enforcement in general. There were times when an innocent person lawyered up, but those times were rarer than one might think.

Liam's head dropped back, his mouth open. He snored about as loudly as one could without having sleep apnea.

It was comical, and Dash couldn't help but laugh.

Raina caught on and laughed too. She had one of those genuine belly laughs that would make even the grumpiest person smile. They both tried to contain their laughter, but the recent stress must have caught up to her because she couldn't stop.

In fact, next thing he knew, she was rolled on her side on the sofa in stiches. It was pure and basic tension relief. By the time she sat up again, she had to wipe the tears from her face.

"That was so good. I needed that. Thank you, Liam," she said and then laughed at her own joke.

It was good to see her smile. And, yes, this was part stress, part exhaustion, but that didn't mean her laughter wasn't real. Dash thought she looked even more beautiful when she relaxed.

He couldn't for the life of him figure out why she wasn't in a relationship. There had to be plenty of guys in line trying to get her to go out with them. Layla shrugged when she brought up the subject of her friend, saying Raina was picky when it came to men. He figured there was a whole lot more to the story, and he surprised himself in realizing he wanted to know the answers. He wanted to know more about Raina and what made her tick.

The fact that she dedicated a good chunk of her salary to her mother's care said all he needed to know about her character. There were far too few female programmers. Based on the code they'd written together just now, he knew how good she was at her job. But then, Layla would get bored hanging around someone who couldn't keep up with her intellectually.

Which made even less sense why Layla had fallen for Calum. The guy had a great job, and most would consider him good looking. He had those two things going for him. But what his sister saw in the man other than those qualities was beyond Dash.

Then again, the guy had to have some charm for Layla to be willing to go out with him.

"What else do you know about my sister's dating history with Calum?" he asked when Raina sat up straight again.

"Only what she told me after the fact," she admitted.

"Did she talk about him? Say why she was infatuated with him in the first place?"

"Not anything specific. She just asked me not to tell anyone when I confronted her about why we weren't spending as much time together. I got the sense she was protecting someone." She flashed her eyes at him. "You know Layla. She's tough on the outside, and it's near impossible to break through her shell. But, man, if you do, you'll never have anyone more loyal on your side," she said.

"To a fault sometimes, I'm afraid," he said.

She nodded. "So few people ever get through. It doesn't happen a lot."

"No. And it's probably best that way. My sister has a tendency to go all in, and I hate how much he hurt her. I could see it in her eyes, and it took all the self-discipline I had not to charge the guy."

"What do you really think about his wife?" she asked.

"Ice queen. She has a lot to lose if she ends up

divorced. She runs with a set of people who would take that as a mark against her. It could potentially cut her out of certain social circles. Someone like her might view her marriage as a contract—one she has every intention of ensuring her husband kept his side of. She might have decided to make sure no monkey business went on between her husband and my sister. Having my sister locked up in jail bans her from the industry and keeps her away from Calum at the office." There was motive. Bitty might have had access to the office, which would give her opportunity. Revenge and protecting one's homelife were two powerful motivators.

"We record who comes in and out of the building. The security footage is always so grainy, though, and we don't record cubicles," she supplied. "There are obvious security risks when it comes to trying to record workstations at a financial firm."

"Miguel already requested the footage, but I agree that I doubt we'll find anything there we don't already know. Always good to be thorough. A few surprises do come up now and then," he said, thinking one of the biggest surprises for him had to do with his growing feelings for Raina.

RAINA HAD ONE question about Calum's wife: "Would she have the contacts to pull off the motorcycle stunt?"

"That's the part that has been bugging me the most. Where would she find someone to do her bidding, even if she did get my sister's password?"

"I doubt Bitty would want to leave a trail that could lead straight back to her. I can't see her trusting a stranger, and I can't see her or her family knowing a hit man." Raina could be wrong. It just didn't seem to fit the image of privileged people in her head. A private detective? Yes, she could easily see them hiring a firm to follow someone around. But she couldn't see them going out to the dark web to hire a hit man. Bitty was too smart to put herself in jeopardy. Right?

Raina could be wrong, but it seemed like Dash agreed with her assessment. Sheldon definitely wouldn't have the kinds of connections that could produce someone like motorcycle guy. But he was smart enough to find the dark web and hire someone from there. Two million dollars was a lot to protect. There was even more at stake once Dash had gotten involved: Sheldon's freedom. Would he calculate the possibility he'd get caught once Layla's brother dug into the case and figure he needed to tilt the scales in his direction? Even the score, so to speak?

"I keep thinking about Sheldon," she said. She gave a quick rundown of her thoughts. "But would he be stupid enough to go after a federal officer? He has to know the stakes go up even higher at that point."

"True. He's young and arrogant. Those are the only two reasons I believe he is still a suspect," he said.

"That pretty much leaves us with Alec," she pointed out.

"I couldn't get facial recognition to work on the guy he was talking to and actually couldn't get a good look at the guy's face anyway. Lip-reading isn't working, even with our program," he said. "I turned it over to headquarters to see if they can do anything with it. Waiting is the worst part of any investigation."

"How do you keep yourself distracted?" She genuinely wanted to know.

"It's just like writing code. I have to take a step back at times, and I accept it as part of the process. Sometimes, the best thing you can do is *not* think about it at all for an hour or two. I sometimes go to the gym or hit the boxing ring and spar with a partner. Anything to distract me for a little while," he admitted. "Nine times out of ten, when I'm done, the answer comes to me."

"That is like coding, actually." She would describe her process as very similar, minus the boxing ring. Instead of the gym, she would go for a run. "I'm a runner, so I would just put in an earbud and play some heavy metal and then take off until I couldn't run anymore. I can't tell you the number of times I get so lost in my head that I forget to double back and end up taking an Uber home because I just don't have the legs anymore."

He smiled and nodded. It was nice to be around someone who understood her quirks.

"Are we going to the office now?" she asked. The sun would be going down before they knew it, and the best time to catch Alec would be on his way home from the office. Catching him off guard would be a good thing.

"I am," he said and gave her a look of apology. "I'm hoping you'll agree to stay here in order to protect your job."

She issued a sharp sigh. "You're right. I know it. But that's hard."

"Losing your job now would add to a list of growing problems. After everything that's happened, I hope you'll seriously consider stepping back. Your mother is safe, and nothing's going to happen to her. I can give you a guarantee there. Not on my watch. As long as Talia is out there, this whole situation becomes even more complicated. And, who knows, she could be responsible for all this. The guy on the motorcycle could have been supposed to run us off the road. Hurt us. Not kill me or you. Or he could have been trying to shoot you and got overzealous. We just don't know, and she would be one of the few people who could pull off something like that. She would have the connections. Believe me."

"If his intent was to capture you, it could have been to get rid of me altogether," she surmised.

"Even more reason for you to stay back under protection," he said.

Raina had to think seriously about it, no matter how much her heart wanted to go with him and fight for Layla. She could be putting his investigation even more at risk.

"How long do I have to decide?" she asked.

Dash checked his watch. "I need an answer now."

She bit her bottom lip and her heart trilled with awareness when his gaze lingered there.

Chapter Twenty

The sun was sinking on the western horizon. Raina had put off making a decision as long as she could. All Dash had to do was catch her gaze, and she knew exactly what he was asking.

"I think you're right about me staying back. I can't risk my job. Not with my mother's care on the line. And that doesn't mean Layla isn't equally important. It's just my mom only has me, whereas Layla has you and your whole unit behind her." She put her hands up, palms out, in the surrender position.

"There's nothing to feel bad about here. You're making the right call for your mother, for you and for Layla. At the end of the day, my sister would be heartbroken if you lost your job and ability to provide for your mother over your association with the investigation. She knows how much you care about her. That's not in question."

"Thank you because I feel like the worst friend in the world for making the call to stand down," she admitted.

He brought his hand up to her chin and lifted it

so her eyes would meet his. "You couldn't be a bad friend if you tried. Besides, you're one of the strongest people I know."

Those words touched her in a deep place—a place she kept locked away for fear one more major hurt might actually break her.

Now, she realized she wasn't giving herself nearly enough credit. She might get knocked down, but she would rise back up. She might get hurt, but she would pick herself up off the floor and keep moving. She might get the wind punched out of her, but she would breathe again. One step at a time. One breath at a time. She would rebuild.

"It means a lot to hear you say that, Dash," she said, locking gazes. Her heart took a hit when he rewarded her with one of his devastating smiles.

"I better head out," he finally said.

"Yes." She didn't want him to miss Alec. "I have Liam here if I need anything."

"Hang tight until I get back." Something passed behind Dash's eyes she couldn't quite pinpoint but hoped was jealousy.

"Be careful," she said.

"Done." The casual smile that followed almost convinced her. It wasn't like he was heading to the store to buy milk. He was going out where they'd been chased and shot at. He changed into a spare pair of joggers and a T-shirt he'd left at his sister's.

Raina expected a full-scale panic to hit as he put on his holster and was surprised when it didn't. In fact, she was breathing easier than she had in longer than she could remember. Learning to let go of everything outside her control was freeing. She had to trust that Dash would be okay. She had to trust his training, his skills and his judgment.

And if that failed him, she had to trust that she would figure out a way to be okay. Because not ever knowing him would be far more tragic, she thought as he put on a jacket and then slipped out the door. Not ever being with someone who could make her heart beat wildly in her chest was settling.

She was done settling even if it meant heartbreak down the line. Would she be able to convince her best friend that Raina could handle both?

DASH FIGURED ALEC would bolt if he caught sight of him. So he turned his back to the entrance of Layla's building and studied his new cell. Again, he'd turned around the camera lens to "selfie" mode.

The sun was setting on another warm late-summer day. Soon enough, there would be a near-constant mist over the city and cooler temperatures. Now, Dash enjoyed the sun on his back.

Patience was the key to surveillance and so much more. It unlocked investigations more often than not. So waiting for a half hour without seeing Alec wasn't a problem for Dash. A thought struck that Alec had left work already. Nothing would surprise Dash at this point. He reached in his pocket and grabbed the now-crumpled paper with Jenny's number on it.

He blocked his number from her caller ID and then made the call.

She picked up on the second ring.

"Hello?" Her voice was hushed, so he figured using her personal cell phone at work was frowned upon.

"Jenny, this is Dash from y—"

"Oh, yes," she said, her voice perking up considerably. "I remember you. I'm actually surprised you called."

"This is a business-related question. Has your boss left work yet?" He hoped she'd give him a pass.

"He never came in today. Can you believe he called in sick? I can count on one hand the number of times that man has called in to work sick in his entire career." She didn't mask her displeasure this wasn't a social call.

"No, I can't believe it. I hope it's nothing contagious," he said, trying to lighten the mood and redirect.

"Oh, no. Nothing like that. Said he has a sinus infection and will be working from home. Might be out for the next few days Do you want me to let him know you're trying to reach him?" she asked, all business now.

"No. I know where to find him. In fact, would you mind doing me a favor?" He pulled on all his charm if he had any. At this point, it was a fifty-fifty toss-up as to how she would respond. He'd upset her with a business question straight out of the gate. And yet she was still on the line. If she had been truly offended, she would have told him where to go by now. No. There was still hope that he would ask her out. Maybe not today but at some point during the investigation. He hated to disappoint her, but he had bigger issues at hand.

"Depends on what it is." Her voice was sultry, and he thought about how she'd let her hips sway back and forth on the way to the elevator. She was pretty, and she had a figure that would drive most men wild.

The problem—and it was a big one—was that she wasn't Raina. Raina had a natural beauty that was unsurpassed. She had just enough curves to go with those mile-long legs. Those were just her external qualities. Where she hit it home was the depth to those sky-blue eyes. Her compassion and loyalty to her mother and his sister enhanced her beautiful package. He'd met far too many women who had a beautiful outer shell. Five minutes into dinner was all it usually took for him to know just how unpleasant the dinner conversation was going to be. And that was only if they met at the restaurant. Generally, he knew how the date was going to go in the first three minutes of conversation.

"How about you keep this conversation between the two of us." He could use his badge and tell her it was a confidential conversation for government reasons, but he figured she might feel obligated to tell her boss. This way, he appealed to her on a personal level.

"And?"

"Were you expecting more?" he asked, knowing full well she wanted a reward.

"I'd like more, if that's what you're offering," she

said in a hushed tone. "I have information about my boss you could probably use."

Well, now he really was interested in where this was going. "How about you share it now?"

"I'd rather not while I'm at work. I could, say, over cocktails," she said.

"How about coffee instead?" he asked. "Right now."

"I think I could get away. With Mr. Kingsley out of the office, he wouldn't know if I routed the office phone to my cell." She seemed to be thinking out loud, so he didn't interrupt her.

Patience.

"Okay. Where would you like to meet?" she asked.

For a split second, he wondered if this was a setup. Taking her to his private coffee spot wasn't ideal. "I'll text you an address in two minutes."

"Okay." There was more than a hint of excitement in her voice now. The second thing he wondered was if this was a ploy to get him out for a drink. Either way, he'd find out soon enough, and his leads had dried up for the moment. Getting Alec's address would be easy, but Miguel would want to send a surveillance team.

Miguel would be right. Plus, Dash needed to visit his sister today. He wanted to get clearance to show her the picture of Alec and the mystery person to see if she recognized him, something he should have been sharp enough to do yesterday. It might be a stretch, trying to ID someone from the back, but it was worth a try. In investigations, he was always looking for the key. Was it Alec?

"I'll hold tight," Jenny said before they ended the call.

He checked the map function of his phone. Luckily, there was a coffee shop every few blocks. He settled on the second-closest one and then sent the address.

Then he sent a text to update the team about Alec not showing up for work before letting them know he was about to meet with the man's admin.

Dash walked the couple of blocks to scout the coffee shop. He wasn't familiar with this one and wanted to scope out the layout. Being outside, the sun warmed his face. There was something about the warmth from the sun that gave him peace. Or was it Raina?

Having spent the past day and a half around her had him rethinking a few aspects of his life. He wanted to help her and her mother. He wanted to give her a place to stay while her apartment was rebuilt. Once they squared his sister away, and he couldn't think of any other option at this point. He couldn't let himself go down the path mentally that Layla would be sent to prison. He'd volunteer to go himself before he'd allow that to happen.

Dash's mind snapped to his parents. All he could think was that he wanted to honor their memories by taking care of Layla. The ironic bit was that Layla could take care of herself in more ways than she couldn't. But he was seeing that she needed him to step up more for her, and he wanted to be the kind of brother she could go to for anything. Not the guy she withheld information from, because he'd had no idea who she was dating, where or when. Could he have talked some sense into her if he'd known? Would it have changed anything?

Maybe not. She had to experience life on her own terms and she'd been clear about keeping working in one bucket, her relationships in another and family separate still. He could only guess at this point and hope that she might have yielded to his experience. He had plenty to draw from. And yet, strangely, all his thoughts recently had centered around one person: Raina.

He wanted to be there for her. He wanted to help make her life easier in any way she would allow. He wanted to take the next step and see where a relationship could go.

Would she be willing to take the next step with him?

Forcing his thoughts back to the investigation, he realized he'd walked the couple of blocks and was across the street from the café where he was to meet Jenny. The front window was a wall of glass. It was one of those bright and airy spots where there were only a half dozen tables needed because most of the business came through mobile orders.

From across the street, he could see all the way to the restroom sign. A public place like this would send the right message to Jenny. This wasn't a date.

Dash counted a cashier and two baristas. After observing for a couple of minutes, he could see that one was dedicated to mobile orders. There was a steady stream of people coming through for a late afternoon pick-me-up. Only one table was occupied by a youngish guy, maybe early twenties, with a headset on and his gaze glued to his laptop.

There was an exit in the back of the building near the restrooms and glass double doors for an entrance. Overall, the place looked copacetic. The constant foot traffic kept the place from feeling too personal.

All in all, this turned out to be the perfect spot for the meetup.

Dash surveyed the area and pinpointed all the places someone could watch him from. That part was less secure. He would pick the table closest to the restrooms where the line would block an outsider's view.

The real threat was from Talia. Had she snapped? Was she behind all this? If she wanted revenge, she would strip him of everyone he cared about before she'd take him out. She would want him to suffer first. She'd covered her vengeful nature early on, but like anything else, an act could only be held up for so long before a break in character showed. The break was the first real peek inside. Dash had been smitten with her. Physically, she was a knockout. She was smart. The disconnect came when he'd realized she was also manipulative.

He'd been infatuated with her and missed a couple of key early warning signs. Again, he was reminded how incredible it was not to have to keep his guard up around Raina. For the first time, he could truly be himself. It was a foreign concept to him—one he could get used to, because he was done with putting on airs.

Was that the reason he'd been losing interest in dating in general?

Jenny appeared across the street, holding on to her handbag a little too tightly. She checked both ways before crossing—not unusual, but there was something foreboding about the tension in her body language. Stiff shoulders. White-knuckle grip on her purse strap.

Something was off.

Dash broke out of line and then slipped out the back door. The alarm sounded as he disappeared in the alley. He thought about the frantic phone call he'd received from Layla after her arrest. It was a rare time she'd lost her composure. She'd sounded distraught and swore she was innocent. She'd promised she would never do such a thing, not ever. She'd sworn on their parents' memory and everything they—and he—had raised her to be that she wasn't guilty, that she'd been framed. But she couldn't figure out who would have wanted to destroy her life. She'd sworn she had no enemies.

From the looks of it, Layla had more enemies than she'd bargained for. Was Jenny involved? Her background check hadn't turned up a whole lot, certainly nothing alarming. Was her seduction routine just that—a routine? Something meant to distract Dash from finding the truth about her or her boss?

Considering office romances weren't all that rare, he could see a picture emerging where Alec and Jenny could be in a secret relationship. Dash pulled an earbud from his pocket, tucked it in his ear and blended in like he was a jogger out for an afternoon run. He circled back to where his vehicle was parked and considered other possibilities for Jenny's involvement. Could Talia have gotten to the admin?

The possibility might be unlikely, but it still had to be considered. He needed to look at this from all angles. He fired off a text to the team, letting them know his meeting turned out to be a bust because she had been sent there by someone. Everything about her body language was forced. The come-on routine was too obvious. He should have seen this coming. To be fair, he'd had his share of women slipping their numbers into his palm over the years. It wasn't his ego talking that made him think she was into him.

Even if she wasn't in a relationship with Alec, she was his admin. Those relationships could become pretty tight, from what he remembered of his time in the corporate world. It was often an admin's job to protect his or her boss, even from spouses.

Another thought occurred. She could be in a relationship with someone else in the office who was trying to set Alec up. There were several possibilities at play here. Staying at the coffee shop wasn't an option, even though part of him wished he could have stuck around for a minute to see if anyone else showed. He would have been too vulnerable there.

Chapter Twenty-One

Raina studied the lines of code. Could she tweak it to make it work and figure out who the mystery guy was? She checked it against Sheldon's and decided he couldn't be ruled out. He would be cunning enough to tweak his code.

There might be half a dozen or so people coming at this investigation from all angles, but that didn't mean she would let up in the least. She might not be able to leave the apartment for safety's sake, but she could still work on the case.

Seeing her friend locked up behind bars when she didn't deserve to be had practically gutted Raina. She wondered how Layla was doing today. This was her thirteenth day behind bars—Thirteen days too many, in Raina's estimation.

What was niggling at the back of her mind about this case?

She kept her eyes glued to the screen, mainly in an attempt to keep her mind busy. Thinking about Dash being out there after what had happened yesterday caused her muscles to tense up. She had to remind herself he was a professional. This was his job, and one he was good at. Actually, *good* was too modest a term. He excelled at this. Plus, he had a team backing him.

He wouldn't make the same mistakes he'd made yesterday. Not Dash. He would learn, tweak and adjust. It was second nature to him.

Raina thought about the office. She should probably check in with the team's admin, Haley, before the workday ended.

She picked up her phone and called.

Haley answered on the second ring. "Hey, Raina."

"Hi. Just checking in to say I'm working from home for a few more days," she said.

"Everything okay?" Haley asked.

"Yes. Fine." Raina hadn't thought about how it might look to the office if her best friend was behind bars and she suddenly stopped showing up for work. "Big project and I need the focus time."

The current open-office setup wasn't conducive to blocking everyone out and focusing. They had a free pass to work from home, even though some preferred to come in. She'd noticed the folks who wanted to come into the office the most were her single coworkers. With no one at home, they preferred coming in so they could be around people. Moms with young kids most often wanted to work from home more, whereas dads in the same situation liked to go in to work. Of course, there were exceptions, but those were the general buckets she'd observed in the workplace.

"Yeah, I get it. Well, it's a ghost town here today. Seems like everyone's out for one reason or another," Haley reported.

"Really? Everyone? Like other departments too?" she asked.

"Yes." Haley lowered her voice. "I know your friend in hedge funds is in trouble, and I'm sorry about that. It seems to have kicked off a wave of people not wanting to come in. I guess with federal investigators watching the office, no one can concentrate on work. Seems like everyone either has a project to work on at home or is out sick."

"Sick?"

"Yeah, your friend's boss called in sick. I was just talking to Jenny about how odd that is," Haley stated.

"Maybe it's the weather," she responded, trying to be casual.

"Too much sunshine, right?" Haley's voice lightened up. "We have no idea what to do with it all."

"Frying our brains," Raina quipped. She was worried about this news. It wasn't sitting right. Why would Alec take off work? The easy answer was that he could control who came in and out of his house, save for the federal agents possessing a warrant. She assumed it was too early for that, or Dash would be all over it. He'd said investigations take time. All she could think was that they didn't have much of it. Every minute Layla sat behind bars was sickening. She couldn't help but wonder where Dash was since Alec hadn't shown up at the office.

"That's so true," Haley said. "But, hey, with everyone out of the office, there was no line at the coffee machine, so I shouldn't exactly complain."

"And you can have all the creamer you want," Raina continued with the banter even though her mind was elsewhere.

"Leave early if I want to." Haley was clearly bored out of her mind.

"Definitely go home early." Raina paused for a beat and then said, "I better get back to it. No seeing the light of day for me while on this project."

"Don't work too hard."

"I'll do my best." Raina ended the call and drummed her fingers. What else could she do besides sit there and wait?

She was surprised that, although she was worried about Dash, she wasn't pacing or literally sick to her stomach like she feared she would be. Could she get past his dangerous job? Her heart said yes. Logic tried to argue, but there was no basis.

If she wanted to think about taking the next step with Dash, she had to accept all the parts of him. She had to come to terms with the fact that he had to work in a job he felt passionate about. Being a federal agent was part of his DNA.

There was another piece of the puzzle that was unknown…Layla. How would she react to learning the news if they decided to move forward? And that was a big *if* at this point. Neither one could deny their chemistry. But taking the next step meant going public.

Her cell buzzed, and it scared the hell out of her

while she was so deep in thought. She checked the screen, half expecting the call to come from her boss.

Dash.

She picked after the first ring. "Hey."

After exchanging greetings, he asked, "What do you know about Jenny?" Hearing his voice on the phone sent warmth rocketing through her. He was safe.

"I know she's Alec's admin. She works in the same department as your sister and that he called in sick today. That's about all," she said.

"Is she married? In a relationship?" he asked.

"Well, not married. There's been gossip on the street that she's seeing someone at work, but everyone tries to keep that stuff under wraps for obvious reasons, so no one knows who it is." She could probably ask Haley just to see what—if anything—she knew. "Why?"

"She made a show of hitting on me when I was in the office yesterday. Forced her personal cell number in my hand as I was leaving," he said.

"Is that right?" The news sent a jealous streak roaring through Raina. It was probably silly to think of Dash in terms of being hers, and yet that's exactly where her heart went with it.

"I tried to meet up with her today…" He paused before adding, "Since Alec called in sick."

"Everyone seems quite taken aback by the news." She needed to redirect her frustration at Dash being hit on. It was to be expected. She only had to take one look at the man to know women would probably line up for the chance to go out with him.

"I thought I could use the number to meet up and get information out of her, and it backfired." He explained to her that he'd just slipped out of the coffee shop.

"The two of them are close, and those rumors about her dating someone at the office—it could easily be him," she said.

"Interesting," he said.

"A picture is emerging, isn't it?" she asked. A few pieces were clicking into place for her.

"Two million dollars would be a nice start toward a new life," he agreed.

"They could go to a lot of places once everything blew over. It must be common knowledge that he isn't happy at the firm considering all the complaints against him from clients. At least in HR circles. No one would be surprised if he quit in a few months. Jenny could follow," she surmised. "She might have assisted in getting Layla's password. It wouldn't be shocking for her to be in Layla's cubicle. This all could have been done right underneath everyone's nose."

"The money trail is the tricky part. Finding the cash would make this a whole lot easier," he said.

"I located the storefront on the web and tried to put a tracer on the back end. I'll keep at it," she said, her mind firing with new ways to approach hacking the code.

"Do you want to come with me to visit Layla?" he asked.

"Yes. Absolutely," she said. "Is it safe?"

"Miguel set it up with Seattle PD to have us followed. He also got approval for me to bring in my phone this time. I'll call you when I'm downstairs in front of the building."

Getting to see Layla would be amazing. She ended the call and ran into the bedroom to find something to wear besides yoga pants and a T-shirt. She rummaged around in the closet while Liam snored from the living room.

Speaking of which, she needed to wake him up and tell him she would be heading downstairs in a few minutes. Give him a chance to get his bearings. She could do that after she threw on some clothes.

Layla's jeans would fit, and she had a short-sleeved sweater Raina had borrowed once before. Her friend probably wouldn't mind if she borrowed those items. Raina dressed in less than a minute and then walked into the living room. She put a hand on Liam's shoulder and gently shook him.

His eyes blinked open, and he sat straight up, reaching behind him for something. A weapon?

"Hey. Hey. Hey." She raised her voice. He seemed to snap out of the fog. He gave a quick headshake.

"Sorry. I dozed off." He put his hands up, palms out, in the surrender position.

"No worries. Just don't shoot me for being the one to wake you."

Liam swiped a hand down his face and then rubbed his chin. "Nope. Not going to hurt you."

"Dash will text when he pulls up out front, and we're heading to visit Layla." She retreated into the master bedroom in part to get away from him and catch her breath—the thought of someone pulling a gun on her half-asleep shot her pulse rate over the top—and in part to put makeup on.

She must look awful, and she wanted to provide a strong front for Layla. A little voice in the back of her head reminded her that Layla didn't care what she looked like. She would be happy just to see her. Or *less angry* might be a better way to put it.

Raina saw, firsthand, how easily Layla snapped to anger and attempted to push everyone away. Not happening. No way, no how. Raina was in this for the long haul and had no plans to walk away from her friend no matter how deep this situation became.

The same little voice also picked that moment to say being with Dash for the past day had been a bright spot in an otherwise crazy and surreal situation. This was also the first time she'd felt truly alive in more years than she cared to remember.

Heart thumping. Blood pumping. Was this what living on the edge felt like?

Raina would never count herself as an adrenaline junkie. She never once thought jumping off a platform with a bungee cord tied to her ankles would be a good time. She never once thought driving a hundred plus miles on the freeway would be her idea of excitement. And yet she had to admit she could see that she hadn't really been living either. Being too careful with every decision she made and never taking a risk seemed just as awful to her right now.

She applied a little makeup from what was available. She found lipstick. Sexy Red. Well, she wasn't so certain about the *sexy* part, but it was red, all right, and it brightened up her face once she'd applied it. She smacked her lips together and then strolled into the next room.

Liam froze midway between the kitchen and the living room, and his jaw nearly dropped to the floor. "Wow," he said, a little louder than he seemed to have intended, judging by his red cheeks.

Her own cheeks were also probably flaming red, but she waved him off. "You're being too nice."

He mumbled something she couldn't quite pick up on and figured was probably best if she didn't.

The text came through from Dash. She held up her phone. "Ready?"

"Let's do this."

Raina walked a step behind Liam. He cleared the hallway before heading to the elevator bank. There was yellow tape across the pair of elevators and a handwritten sign that read, *out of order.*

Raina groaned. "Are you kidding me?" For a high-tech building, the elevators sure went out a lot. Considering the prices, Layla should have been getting a walk-the-stairs discount, especially considering the fact that she was on the twenty-third floor.

"Does this happen a lot?" Liam asked.

"Afraid so," Raina said.

"Okay. Stick close behind me and we'll take the stairs," he said.

"Better down than up." She'd done both. It was one of many reasons she wouldn't pay these sky-high rent prices—the first of which was that she couldn't afford them anyway. Even if she could, she preferred to keep her feet closer to the ground. Strangely—and it was probably just the gorgeous water view—she felt right at home at Dash's apartment. Thinking of home caused her stomach to clench. She still hadn't checked on the damage.

"Can't argue that point," Liam agreed.

The stairwell was narrow, and the ceilings were low. No matter how many times she'd made this trip, the walls felt like they were closing in, and her chest tightened every time she was in here.

Liam was broad, and he was almost shoulder to shoulder against the walls. When he extended his arms, his elbows scraped against them. Once they got down to the floors with amenities, the stairwell opened up considerably. The residence floors were tight.

She kept her eyes on the floor. Focusing on the steps helped her get down without too much anxiety.

As she passed a door on the fourteenth floor, it opened and she was yanked inside a hallway. A hand came over her eyes as she was slammed into the wall face-first. She heard a noise like metal scraping against metal, and then everything went black.

Chapter Twenty-Two

Dash sat in front of his sister's building with the SUV engine idling, waiting for Raina and Liam to emerge. The fact that it had been four minutes and thirty-two seconds since she'd confirmed his text had him on pins and needles.

Gut instinct honed by years of experience caused him to cut the engine and make a run inside. He breezed through the modern-style lobby as the phone in his hand buzzed.

"What's wrong?" he immediately asked Liam after checking caller ID.

"They got her"

"Who got her? What happened?" Dash stopped in front of the elevator doors.

"Fourteenth floor. I'm locked in the stairwell," Liam informed him. "Elevator's broken."

Dash pushed the button, and a set of doors opened. "Says who?"

"Access was blocked from the twenty-th—"

Liam cursed before shuffling sounds came through

the line. He was, no doubt, gunning toward a different floor so he could take the elevator.

Since there was no movement, he assumed she was still on fourteen. Dash stepped inside and drew his weapon. He pushed the appropriate button. "Did you get the other one?"

"I'm in. I'll be going down one floor." Liam was closer, so his doors would open first.

"Be careful," he warned.

"Of course." The anguish and frustration in Liam's voice came through loud and clear. He wouldn't take this lightly.

Dash's pulse was through the roof as he tapped his toe, waiting for the elevator to reach its destination. This wasn't the time to review his mistakes, but the critical one—and the reason he blamed himself for Raina's abduction—was that they'd stayed in the building too long. He should have kept her on the move. He'd fallen into a false sense of security.

"On fourteen. Doors opening." A few seconds passed. "Clear."

The minute the bell dinged, Dash surveyed the landing and immediately located Liam. Back to back, they moved down the long hallway.

A door opened as they moved past it. A startled-looking jogger seemed to change her mind.

"Federal agent," Dash said quietly.

She retreated instantly.

They listened for any sounds of struggle. Nothing. There were eight apartments on each floor in this tower, four on each side. Liam and Dash moved down the hallway methodically, listening carefully at each door.

The perp had to know they would be on the floor by now. The thought Raina could already be dead wasn't something Dash could accept. It was in that moment he realized how deep his feelings were for her. The thought of anything happening to her was more than a gut punch—it threatened to rip his heart to shreds.

When this was over and she was safe—and that was the only outcome he could consider—he intended to see if she felt the same way, if there was any chance they could be together on any terms. Layla would come around. She had to.

At the last set of doors, Liam got a hit. They switched positions so that Dash faced the door. He fired off a text with the address to Miguel with a request for help. The cavalry would arrive in a matter of minutes. But would it be too late for Raina? Was she even in the room?

Heart pounding, chest threatening to crack open, he used his police-raid knock.

"Federal agents, open up," Dash said in his loud authoritative voice.

The music that had been thumping from apartment 1407 came to a grinding halt. Anyone who was home on this floor was probably glued to their peephole right now, which didn't matter as long as they stayed inside where they'd be safe.

Dash fired off three more of those wall-shaking knocks.

"Open the door right now."

"I'm willing to negotiate," came the voice he recognized as Alec's. He couldn't possibly have pulled off tricking Liam on his own, which meant there were at least two people on the other side of the door. Three, counting Raina.

Dash wasn't a hostage negotiator, so he texted Miguel. "How about you come out here and we'll talk."

"No, thank you," came the muffled response. Alec?

"Send out your hostage." Dash figured he was dealing with an amateur, and that would work to his advantage. He might as well go ahead and ask for what he wanted straight out of the gate.

"Sorry. Not happening," Alec said. He cleared his throat. He was trying to mask his uncertainty by sounding commanding.

"I need to verify the hostage is alive," Dash said.

"She is."

"Your word isn't good enough, Alec." Dash needed Alec to realize he knew exactly who he was speaking to. "I need proof. Let her speak to me."

"She can't right now."

"Then we have nothing to talk about. But I'll tell you this…" Dash had to make a bold move so Alec would be certain he wasn't going to walk out of here unless Dash said so. "In about five minutes, this block will be surrounded by Seattle PD. Around the same time, this building will be crawling with federal agents. There will be more law enforcement on this floor than bees around a hive. So, we can do this your way, which will lead to you being taken by force into custody, or we can do this my way, which will lead to your peaceful arrest. Either way, you're going to jail."

"Not an option." Alec's voice was a bit shakier now.

"What did you think was going to happen, Alec?"

"I want safe passage out of the building, or I'll kill her." He was trying to force confidence. This was the first real sign that Raina was alive. In boxing terms, Dash had Alec against the ropes.

"Kill her and you have no bargaining tool. That wouldn't just be reckless, it would be stupid," Dash reasoned.

There were a few beats of silence before a fist slammed against the other side of the door.

"Who is in there with you, Alec?" Dash asked.

"That's not your concern."

Dash's cell indicated a text had come through. The message was from Miguel.

Sending up a chopper.

"Time is ticking, Alec. The longer I stand here, the hungrier I get. Do you know what that means?"

"I don't care."

"Yes, you do. Because when I get hungry, I'm a son of a bitch to deal with. And that means I'll rip this door down with my bare hands if I have to," Dash said.

More of that silence.

Another text came through.

Building maintenance is on the way up.

The elevator dinged.

"Guess what else, Alec?" Dash continued. "Maintenance is stepping off the elevator now. He has a key on his key ring that will open the door. If you're seen as cooperating, the jury might go lighter on your sentence."

The guy didn't realize it yet, but he'd already lost.

Dash just wished he knew who else was on the other side of the door with him. Was it motorcycle guy?

"Three minutes have passed. That means Seattle's finest is closing in," Dash warned. "Open up before it gets worse."

A few tense seconds passed before the dead-bolt lock clicked. The door opened a crack, and footsteps could be heard backing away. Not a good sign.

Dash's heart was in his throat. He glanced at Liam, who gave him a look of solidarity.

Dash wasn't lying. Agents would swarm the building soon. Seattle PD was setting up a perimeter. The only thing he'd fudged was the timing.

A guy in jeans and a clean white shirt emerged from the elevator. He had a ring of keys in his hands. A few seconds too late, Dash thought.

Dash shook his head and put his hand up to warn the maintenance man to stay back. He pointed toward the elevators, and Dash nodded as he stepped a foot just inside the door. No one could close it now.

With Liam behind him, Dash flattened his back against the wall and took the first step inside. "Make sure your hands are where I can see them, Alec."

No response.

Dash's stomach dropped.

"Alec?"

Again, nothing.

The layout of the apartment should be similar to Layla's, so Dash risked a step inside. There was no cover in the entryway, but he had a straight line of sight all the way to the window. A chopper hovered out the window.

"Do you see that, Alec? They're here for you," Dash said. "A team is on its way up via the elevator and the stairs. There are no exits."

Dash pushed a little deeper into the apartment as a drape blew toward him from the Juliet balcony, where Alec was holding an unresponsive Raina as he leaned against the rail.

One of the most basic rules of law enforcement dictated never running toward an injured person. He was trained to follow protocol for a reason, to save his life. So he had to fight every instinct he had not to charge toward Alec.

"Bring her inside," Dash said calmly, although his heart was pounding fifty miles an hour.

"No." There was a hysterical quality to Alec's voice now.

"What are you going to do? Throw her over? I'm

here. Cops are everywhere. You don't want to add murder to the list of crimes. What you've done so far is something you can eventually walk away from. Kill her and it's game over." Dash's finger hovered on the trigger. He had a clean shot, and yet he couldn't risk Raina being tossed over the edge. Despite what it looked like on TV, there was only one shot that stopped a person in their tracks. All others took a few minutes for the brain to catch up. If someone was charging at the shooter, they would continue to charge.

Dash was skilled with a gun. He wouldn't take the risk.

"Shoot me and she dies," Alec said, his voice a little more hysterical. He moved his right hand from around Raina's hip, and Dash immediately saw the weapon aimed at him.

Seemingly out of nowhere, a female figure clad in all black leaped toward Alec. Her swift movements were so elegant and graceful he immediately knew who she was: Talia.

A scream ripped from her throat as Alec fired. She knocked the gun loose from Alec's hand. Raina dropped onto the floor with a thud. Dash didn't waste a second, he lunged toward Alec as Liam made a move for the weapon, which slid across the wood with a scraping sound.

Dash wrestled Alec to the floor and was on top of his chest, squeezing his arms at his sides with the leverage of his thighs.

Talia rolled over to them like a gator with prey in its teeth.

"Freeze, Talia," Dash said. He aimed his weapon in her direction in time to see blood pooling on the floor where she'd stopped three feet away from him.

"She's pathetic," Talia growled.

"You're bleeding."

The thunder of footsteps sounded in the hallway. The cavalry had arrived.

"In the living room. I'm armed," Dash shouted, unsure if this would be local PD or a member of his team.

"What did you do to her?" Dash asked Talia.

"Why should I tell you?" she asked, defiance in her tone.

"Because I'm in love with her." There. He said it. He meant every word. "And if she'll have me, I plan to ask her to marry me."

A gut-wrenching cry tore from Talia's throat. "Why? Why not me?" She balled her fists and thrust them in the air. "Why not me, Dash? Tell me."

"The heart wants what it wants, Talia." It was all he could say. His wanted Raina.

Talia did a back roll as a local cop stormed the room, weapon drawn. His partner came in right behind him.

"Hands in the air, Talia. Don't give them a reason to shoot," Dash ordered.

Talia hesitated before slowly bringing her hands up. Blood dripped from her right elbow, and her skin had paled.

"She's shot. See that she gets medical attention." Make no mistake about it, Dash owed her his life. Because she'd acted, he could save Raina. "This man is responsible for stealing two million dollars. He took a hostage, and he threatened a federal officer." Dash eased his grip, twisted Alec onto his face and jerked his hands behind his back. "Read him his rights and lock him up."

"Yes, sir," the first officer said. The second zip-cuffed Talia as Dash practically launched himself toward Raina.

Liam was already there beside her, and he was giving her something that looked a lot like smelling salts. She wrinkled her nose and blinked her eyes. She jerked her head back and twisted up her face.

"Dash." His name sounded like heaven on her tongue.

"I'm here." And he had no plans to leave.

Chapter Twenty-Three

The bed was warm, the covers soft. Raina was pretty certain most people didn't get to sleep in a room that felt more like a luxury hotel than a hospital. Dash had insisted she let him cover the bill.

She'd been in and out of sleep for a couple of hours before she finally felt awake enough to sit up on her own. The second she stirred, Dash was by her side.

"Hey," he said. His masculine voice washed over and through her.

"Hi there."

He stood next to her bed, the light behind him creating a halo effect around his head. He was her angel, all right.

"How are you feeling?" He covered her hand with his, and that familiar and comforting electricity jolted through her.

"Better when I look at you." She smiled. It was corny, but it elicited a devastating grin from him.

"I was hoping you'd say something like that, because I don't plan on leaving anytime soon."

Her heart squeezed at the thought of him leaving at all.

"What happened? The last couple of hours are a blur," she admitted. Her memories were hazy and felt more like a dream than reality.

"Alec stole the money because he was tired of being passed over for promotion. Miguel discovered his nickname was Phish, and that led to linking him to the storefront on the dark web. Alec talked Jenny into slipping a thumb drive in Layla's computer, which stole Layla's password. Once he learned she'd been having an affair with a married man he didn't mind letting her take the fall for a crime she didn't commit. Her erratic behavior gave him an easy out," he explained.

"Who was the guy from the lobby?" she asked.

"Someone Alec planned to invest in once he got the money safely filtered through his storefront. The start-up would be a way to clean the money," he said.

"And Sheldon?" she asked.

"He broke into the system and stole social security numbers, according to Liam. Sheldon wanted revenge. He just hadn't decided what he was going to do with them yet. He will be prosecuted for his crime," he said. "There's a fine line between genius and criminal."

Raina had seen that more than once.

"What about my mom and my apartment?" she asked.

"Both have been taken care of. Your mom is safely back at her rehab facility. She slept through most of the time she was off property. She is asking to see you," Dash said before frowning. "Not much was salvageable in the apartment. What the fire didn't destroy, water did." He paused. "I'm sorry about that."

"It's not your fault," she defended.

"It is Talia's and she never would have gone after you if not for me."

"What about Talia? In my dream, she was there."

"I was tracking Alec, and she tailed me. Once she figured out who I was after, she saw an opportunity to get back at me through hurting Layla and then you. Alec needed you out of the picture, so she helped him but said he panicked once the plan started unraveling and news the motorcycle guy she'd hired almost killed us both. Alec and Jenny stole the money and planned to start a new life with it. Both wanted out of the firm but neither is a career criminal, so they started cracking under the pressure. Once Talia figured out what was going on, she tried to strike up a bargain. Deliver me and she would help them."

"She must really hate me," Raina said.

"I doubt you're her favorite person, but that's only because I love you."

She blinked at him, unsure she'd just heard right. "Excuse me. What did you just say?"

"That I love you. And I do, Raina. I've never met anyone who makes me feel the way you do. I've never met anyone I couldn't walk away from without feeling like a hole had been punched in my chest," he admitted, and for a split second, he looked incredibly vulnerable. "So what do you think? Do you feel the same?"

Is that a real question?

"I'm deeply in love with you, Dash. I can't imagine loving anyone more, because what we have is special. I was afraid that I couldn't handle the thought of anything happening to you in your job. But I choose not to live in fear anymore. Being afraid has been holding me back from really being alive, and I want to give you all of me," she said.

His response came in the form of a tender kiss.

"But there's another person in our lives to consider. There's no question that I feel the same way about you. But Layla's important, and I doubt she would give her blessing." Raina gasped because it suddenly sank in that Alec was behind bars. Was her friend in there with him? "Speaking of Layla, is she out? I can't believe I didn't ask about her first. What kind of person am I?"

Just as shame nearly dragged Raina under, Layla stepped out of the shadows. "One who risks her life to save mine."

"Layla." Tears welled in Raina's eyes at seeing her friend out of jail, free. "Come here."

Layla crossed her arms over her chest and shook her head.

"I can't. Not until my brother asks the question he's working up to ask," Layla said, and then her face broke into a wide smile.

Dash got down on one knee at Raina's bedside.

"Raina, I'll never love anyone as much as I love

you. What we have is special and real, and I don't want to lose you ever again." He paused for a beat as Raina's heart hammered in her throat. "Would you do me the incredible honor of marrying me?"

She didn't have to think about it for a second. All she had to do was look over at her best friend, who nodded.

"Yes, Dash. I will marry you. I'm hopelessly in love with you, and I want to start forever as a family."

Dash pushed up enough to kiss her, soft and tender.

Layla cleared her throat. "Excuse me. I have something to say."

She moved beside her brother, who made room for her.

"I already feel like we're sisters, so I can't wait to make it official," Layla said.

"You're already my family, Layla. We don't need a piece of paper for that," Raina said, then added, "But I'm marrying your hot brother."

"Oh no. Did you just call my brother 'hot'?" Layla laughed. Raina laughed. Dash laughed.

Raina couldn't wait to make this family official. With Dash, she'd found her place. She'd found home.

Epilogue

Dash rolled up his wrinkled sleeves. He picked up a pen from the top of his desk and absently rolled it around his fingers. It was late, and he had a fiancée to get home to. As much as he respected Raina and Layla's girls' night in, he couldn't wait to see his future bride.

He closed down his computer and pushed to standing, stretching out the muscles that were sore from sitting too long in his chair.

A few coworkers were still in the building, but he figured he could slip out without too much fanfare… until Lorelai came running past his desk in tears. *What the…?* Lorelai wasn't a crier—at all.

In the next second, Madeline came rushing past—chasing after Lorelai, no doubt. Dash muttered a curse, wishing he could just leave, despite knowing he couldn't do that without assuring she'd be okay.

Liam came by a second later, and Dash figured the two of them had had a fight.

"Hey, what's going on with Lorelai? She came past here looking upset," Dash said.

"Wedding stuff." Liam shook his head. "You don't want to hear about this. You're still glowing from your proposal, man."

"Try me out."

"Okay. If you're sure about this. Weddings can get pretty hairy," Liam warned.

"Let's hear it."

"My mom keeps calling. She's upset because Lorelai isn't including her enough." He issued a sharp sigh. "I can't have my mom constantly calling me, so I asked my bride-to-be if she could ask my mom's opinion once in a while."

"How'd that go over?" Seemed like a rookie mistake to Dash.

"She started crying and said everyone is mad at her—her sisters, her maid of honor—because she's supposedly being a bridezilla," he confessed.

"She probably just wants everything to be perfect."

"Is there ever such a thing?" Liam had a point. He continued, "After I brought it up, she said she would try, but that the wedding somehow felt off-balance to her now. She said maybe we should rethink this whole situation."

"That's intense," Dash said.

"Yeah. I love her. I know we're meant to be together. When you know, you just know. Right?"

Dash nodded. "That's how it worked for me."

Miguel came down the hallway as Lorelai and Madeline came back. They stopped at Dash's cubicle. Lorelai didn't lift her gaze to meet Liam's.

Bottle of champagne in hand, Miguel requested someone grab a few cups. "It's time to celebrate the successful end to a tough case."

"Hear, hear." Dash would definitely toast to his sister's freedom. The cherry on the cake was that he'd found his future bride in the process.

And he couldn't wait to start a family.

* * * * *

*Look for the next two books in
the Behavioral Analysis Unit series,*
Tracing a Kidnapper *by Juno Rushdan
in September and* Trapping a Terrorist
*by New York Times best-selling author
Caridad Piñeiro in October.*

And don't miss the previous book in the series:

Profiling a Killer *by Nichole Severn*

*Available now wherever
Harlequin Intrigue books are sold!*

**WE HOPE YOU ENJOYED
THIS BOOK FROM**

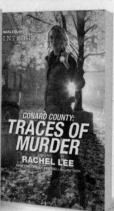

Seek thrills. Solve crimes. Justice served.

Dive into action-packed stories that will keep you
on the edge of your seat. Solve the crime
and deliver justice at all costs.

6 NEW BOOKS AVAILABLE EVERY MONTH!

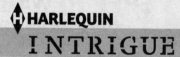
#2019 TRACING A KIDNAPPER
Behavioral Analysis Unit • by Juno Rushdan
FBI agent Madeline Striker's new case involves locating the kidnapped daughter of tech CEO Jackson Rhodes. The kidnap specialist's fierce determination to rescue Jackson's child forges a powerful bond between them, even as a vindictive enemy threatens the child's life.

#2020 SURVIVING THE TRUTH
The Saving Kelby Creek Series • by Tyler Anne Snell
When Willa Tate presents Detective Kenneth Gray with a buried box containing evidence of a thirty-five-year-old crime, he knows his newly formed task force will leave no stone unturned to find answers. But protecting Willa and righting past wrongs pits the dogged cop against a killer desperate to silence the truth forever.

#2021 K-9 RECOVERY
STEALTH: Shadow Team • by Danica Winters
The latest assignment for STEALTH operative Elle Spade and her K-9 partner, Daisy, not only involves locating and rescuing a toddler, but also forces her to work with Sergeant Grant Anders. The no-nonsense cop has just joined the search, and as they make a desperate effort to find the child alive, and with Daisy in the lead, they follow a sinister trail that leads to murder.

#2022 FOR THE DEFENSE
A Raising the Bar Brief • by Maggie Wells
Deputy Lori Cabrera is shocked to discover that a powerful local businessman is a front for a drug-trafficking ring tucked away in her own rural Georgia community. It figures his defense attorney is none other than the distractingly handsome Simon Wingate. Is it possible the big-city attorney is putting more than his heart on the line to see that justice is served?

#2023 MISSING AT CHRISTMAS
West Investigations • by K.D. Richards
Private investigator Shawn West is stunned when the attack victim he rescues is Addy Williams—the one woman he never forgot. She's turning a quiet upstate New York town inside out to bring her missing sister home by Christmas. Can they work together to find Addy's sister...or are they already too late?

#2024 DEAD IN THE WATER
by Janice Kay Johnson
Claire Holland is terrified when a kayaking adventure accidentally intercepts a smuggling operation and her friend is gunned down. But before she can escape, Claire witnesses someone getting shot and falling overboard. Undercover DEA agent Adam Taylor is still alive but badly injured. Has Claire saved a handsome hero's life...just to find her own in jeopardy?

Love Harlequin romance?

DISCOVER.

Be the first to find out about promotions,
news and exclusive content!

Facebook.com/HarlequinBooks

Twitter.com/HarlequinBooks

Instagram.com/HarlequinBooks

Pinterest.com/HarlequinBooks

YouTube.com/HarlequinBooks

ReaderService.com

EXPLORE.

Sign up for the Harlequin e-newsletter and
download a free book from any series at
TryHarlequin.com

CONNECT.

Join our Harlequin community to
share your thoughts and connect
with other romance readers!
Facebook.com/groups/HarlequinConnection